SEEKING RETRIBUTION
DI SARA RAMSEY
BOOK TWENTY-THREE

M A COMLEY

Copyright © 2024 by M A Comley

All rights reserved.

No part of this book may be reproduced in any form or by any electronic or mechanical means, including information storage and retrieval systems, without written permission from the author, except for the use of brief quotations in a book review.

ACKNOWLEDGMENTS

Special thanks as always go to @studioenp for their superb cover design expertise.

My heartfelt thanks go to my wonderful editor Emmy, and my proofreaders Joseph and Barbara for spotting all the lingering nits.

Thank you also to my amazing ARC Group who help to keep me sane during this process.

To Mary, gone, but never forgotten. I hope you found the peace you were searching for my dear friend. I miss you each and every day.

ALSO BY M A COMLEY

Blind Justice (Novella)

Cruel Justice (Book #1)

Mortal Justice (Novella)

Impeding Justice (Book #2)

Final Justice (Book #3)

Foul Justice (Book #4)

Guaranteed Justice (Book #5)

Ultimate Justice (Book #6)

Virtual Justice (Book #7)

Hostile Justice (Book #8)

Tortured Justice (Book #9)

Rough Justice (Book #10)

Dubious Justice (Book #11)

Calculated Justice (Book #12)

Twisted Justice (Book #13)

Justice at Christmas (Short Story)

Prime Justice (Book #14)

Heroic Justice (Book #15)

Shameful Justice (Book #16)

Immoral Justice (Book #17)

Toxic Justice (Book #18)

Overdue Justice (Book #19)

Unfair Justice (a 10,000 word short story)

Irrational Justice (a 10,000 word short story)

Seeking Justice (a 15,000 word novella)

Caring For Justice (a 24,000 word novella)

Savage Justice (a 17,000 word novella)

Justice at Christmas #2 (a 15,000 word novella)

Gone in Seconds (Justice Again series #1)

Ultimate Dilemma (Justice Again series #2)

Shot of Silence (Justice Again series #3)

Taste of Fury (Justice Again series #4)

Crying Shame (Justice Again series #5)

See No Evil (Justice Again #6)

To Die For (DI Sam Cobbs #1)

To Silence Them (DI Sam Cobbs #2)

To Make Them Pay (DI Sam Cobbs #3)

To Prove Fatal (DI Sam Cobbs #4)

To Condemn Them (DI Sam Cobbs #5)

To Punish Them (DI Sam Cobbs #6)

To Entice Them (DI Sam Cobbs #7)

To Control Them (DI Sam Cobbs #8)

To Endanger Lives (DI Sam Cobbs #9)

To Hold Responsible (DI Sam Cobbs #10)

To Catch a Killer (DI Sam Cobbs #11)

To Believe The Truth (DI Sam Cobbs #12)

To Blame Them (DI Sam Cobbs #13)

Forever Watching You (DI Miranda Carr thriller)

Wrong Place (DI Sally Parker thriller #1)

No Hiding Place (DI Sally Parker thriller #2)

Cold Case (DI Sally Parker thriller#3)

Deadly Encounter (DI Sally Parker thriller #4)

Lost Innocence (DI Sally Parker thriller #5)
Goodbye My Precious Child (DI Sally Parker #6)
The Missing Wife (DI Sally Parker #7)
Truth or Dare (DI Sally Parker #8)
Where Did She Go? (DI Sally Parker #9)
Sinner (DI Sally Parker #10)
The Good Die Young (DI Sally Parker #11)
Coping Without You (DI Sally Parker #12)
Could it be him? (DI Sally Parker #13)
Web of Deceit (DI Sally Parker Novella)
The Missing Children (DI Kayli Bright #1)
Killer On The Run (DI Kayli Bright #2)
Hidden Agenda (DI Kayli Bright #3)
Murderous Betrayal (Kayli Bright #4)
Dying Breath (Kayli Bright #5)
Taken (DI Kayli Bright #6)
The Hostage Takers (DI Kayli Bright Novella)
No Right to Kill (DI Sara Ramsey #1)
Killer Blow (DI Sara Ramsey #2)
The Dead Can't Speak (DI Sara Ramsey #3)
Deluded (DI Sara Ramsey #4)
The Murder Pact (DI Sara Ramsey #5)
Twisted Revenge (DI Sara Ramsey #6)
The Lies She Told (DI Sara Ramsey #7)
For The Love Of… (DI Sara Ramsey #8)
Run for Your Life (DI Sara Ramsey #9)
Cold Mercy (DI Sara Ramsey #10)
Sign of Evil (DI Sara Ramsey #11)

Indefensible (DI Sara Ramsey #12)
Locked Away (DI Sara Ramsey #13)
I Can See You (DI Sara Ramsey #14)
The Kill List (DI Sara Ramsey #15)
Crossing The Line (DI Sara Ramsey #16)
Time to Kill (DI Sara Ramsey #17)
Deadly Passion (DI Sara Ramsey #18)
Son Of The Dead (DI Sara Ramsey #19)
Evil Intent (DI Sara Ramsey #20)
The Games People Play (DI Sara Ramsey #21)
Revenge Streak (DI Sara Ramsey #22)
Seeking Retribution (DI Sara Ramsey #23)
I Know The Truth (A Psychological thriller)
She's Gone (A psychological thriller)
Shattered Lives (A psychological thriller)
Evil In Disguise – a novel based on True events
Deadly Act (Hero series novella)
Torn Apart (Hero series #1)
End Result (Hero series #2)
In Plain Sight (Hero Series #3)
Double Jeopardy (Hero Series #4)
Criminal Actions (Hero Series #5)
Regrets Mean Nothing (Hero series #6)
Prowlers (Di Hero Series #7)
Sole Intention (Intention series #1)
Grave Intention (Intention series #2)
Devious Intention (Intention #3)
Cozy mysteries

Murder at the Wedding

Murder at the Hotel

Murder by the Sea

Death on the Coast

Death By Association

Merry Widow (A Lorne Simpkins short story)

It's A Dog's Life (A Lorne Simpkins short story)

A Time To Heal (A Sweet Romance)

A Time For Change (A Sweet Romance)

High Spirits

The Temptation series (Romantic Suspense/New Adult Novellas)

Past Temptation

Lost Temptation

Clever Deception (co-written by Linda S Prather)

Tragic Deception (co-written by Linda S Prather)

Sinful Deception (co-written by Linda S Prather)

For Mum, you never let me down, thank you for giving me the tools and the backing to begin this incredible journey. Thank you for always believing in me.

Miss you every minute of every day, you truly were a Mum in a million. My heart, my soul.

PROLOGUE

The van pulled up outside the office block and waited. They were early, and the gang members were nervous. This was the first time they'd ever done something as unlawful as this, and it showed in their eyes.

Their target appeared in the doorway. He was alone and glanced around him but failed to see the van, or if he did, he chose to ignore it and crossed the road to the car park opposite.

"This is it," the driver said. "It's now or never. Are you ready for this?"

The other two occupants nodded, and each of them rubbed their gloved hands together.

"Let's do this."

The driver started the van and eased it around the edge of the building and blocked the exit to the car park, knowing there was only one way in and out. It was all part of the plan they'd spent ages formulating.

"Have you got all the equipment to hand? You know what to do, don't you?"

"Yes, we've been over this a gazillion times. This is where

the talking ends and the actions begin to take shape. Don't worry about us, we've got this."

The driver was unsure about the member of the gang who had kept quiet, though. "Are you ready?"

A sharp nod came in response, followed by a huge gulp.

"There's no turning back once we get our plan underway. Any doubts, now is your chance to air them."

"There's no going back. We're with you on this every step of the way. Now stop talking."

The driver fixed their gaze on the man fast approaching his vehicle. "Almost there now."

The other two gathered the rope, hood and injection and awaited further instructions by the back door.

"He's almost with you, another ten feet. As soon as he blasts his horn at me, that's your cue to surprise him."

His car wound its way from the back of the car park to the exit and paused for a second or two. Then the sound of the horn came.

The driver shouted, "Go, go, go. You've got two minutes to make this happen, don't let me down. I'll keep an eye out and join you once I think it's safe."

They flung the back door open, and two people leapt out. The driver turned to face the action, rather than watch it all unfold in the wing mirror.

The man got out of his vehicle, started shouting and gesticulating with a clenched fist as soon as the two people appeared but thought better about making a scene, probably because his assailants were wearing balaclavas, their intent clear.

Considering it was the first time either of them had done this before, the manoeuvre was carried out with precision and ease. Once the man was injected, he slumped to the ground.

The driver jumped out of the driver's seat and ran to the rear to help the others throw him in. "Well done, we did it."

"Not yet, but we're on the way to success. Give us a hand getting him secured."

Between them, they made light work of the task and had the man tied up in the seat they had brought with them.

The driver left the others, hopped back into the front and drove to the location where they would be holding the man for the next few days at least.

It would all be about getting a confession out of him now. They appreciated it would be far from easy, but with the well-laid-out plan to guide them, they knew they were well on their way to achieving their goal.

CHAPTER 1

A few weeks earlier

THE BLACK CAT nightclub was a relatively new place for the people of Hereford to hang out. It used to be a warehouse, on the outskirts of the city, until a wealthy developer saw the potential in the site to open an exclusive, invitation-only venue. Six months later, and after the initial enthusiasm had worn off for the nightspot and the millionaire entrepreneur owner had dropped the exclusivity aspect, along with the extortionate prices, the venue was buzzing at eleven-thirty on a Thursday evening.

"Let's get a drink from the bar and then grab a table over on the far side of the dance floor where it's a little quieter," Chelsey suggested.

"Why don't I find the table and you and Tamzin order the drinks?" Polly shouted back over the din of the pounding beat.

Chelsey nodded and gave her a thumbs-up. "What do you want?"

"A mojito will do, thanks. I'll get the next round in."

Chelsey swept her long auburn hair over her right shoulder. "Don't worry about it, I know you're good for it."

She approached the shiny mirrored bar with her friend, Tamzin, not far behind her. They waited patiently to be served by the barman at the end who was busy chatting up the young woman he was trying to impress with his cocktail shaker in one hand and a bottle of vodka in the other.

"Jesus, what does a girl have to do to get attention around here?"

"I'll go and tell him to shake a leg." Tamzin grumbled and went to walk away but Chelsey caught her by the arm, surprising her.

"Be kind. The last thing we need is you mouthing off and getting us thrown out of here."

Tamzin's lower jaw dropped open briefly then clamped shut again. "As if I would! What do you take me for? I know when to behave myself, it's not difficult."

Chelsey rolled her eyes. "Past experience tells me otherwise, but carry on, don't let me stop you. And watch the claws on the girl, too. Seems to me she's put in a lot of effort to get the barman's attention, only for you to come along and spoil things for her."

"Jesus, do you want that frigging drink or don't you? We're entitled to be served in a timely manner. This place is filling up quickly, he shouldn't be trying to impress the punters with his deft touch with a cocktail shaker, he can do that in his own time."

"Whatever," Chelsey called after her. She rested her back against the bar, her gaze flitting between her two friends. Polly had found a decent seat, as promised, and had spread her belongings on the plush seats around her. Tamzin, on the other hand, had managed to raise the hackles on the young woman intent on flirting with the barman and was receiving an evil glare for her troubles.

The woman was gesticulating angrily with her arms. You didn't have to hear the conversation to know how well it was going.

Shit, leave well alone, Tamzin. When are you going to learn that patience is a virtue that has thus far evaded you?

Tamzin said a few choice words and turned her back on the seething punter. The barman followed her back up the bar to attend to their needs.

"Sorry about that, ladies. Now, what can I get you? In other words, name your poison and I'll be sure to deliver."

"Promptly, I hope," Chelsey said, her smile taut, letting him know she meant business.

"Of course."

"In that case, we'll have three of your finest mojitos."

He set off down to the other end of the bar again.

"What a tosser. Don't tell me he's only got the one shaker?" Tamzin complained.

"Give him a chance. Maybe he favours that one over the others behind the bar. He's coming now. He's probably learnt his lesson."

"We'll see."

Chelsey and Tamzin watched on as he skilfully poured the contents into the shaker and prepared the cocktail glasses. He added a slice of lime around the sugar-encrusted edge and tipped the contents of the blended white rum, lime juice, sugar, soda water and mint leaves into the three glasses and pushed them across the bar towards Chelsey who paid him.

"Thanks, I hope they're worth the wait."

"They're the best in town, I assure you," he responded and totted up the round on the till. He returned with Chelsey's change of a couple of pounds and placed the money in her open palm. His gaze drifted to the glass on the counter, a tip jar sign tented in front of it.

Chelsey grinned and chose to ignore the enormous hint. "Thanks."

He glared at her, his smile fixed in place, and she and Tamzin collected the glasses and negotiated the dance floor to join Polly at their table.

"Problem?" Polly accepted the drink from Chelsey.

"Nothing we couldn't handle between us. Nice table. Cheers, girls. Here's to a fantastic night. We all deserve it after what we've been through lately."

The three of them sipped at their drinks and sighed.

"Not half. Have you seen Greg lately, Tamzin?" Polly asked.

"Not since I threatened him when he showed up at the gym the other week. I think having Butch by my side while I told him what I thought of him did the trick of eventually getting the point across."

"Ah yes, the ever useful Butch with his powerful guns and rippling pecs," Polly said. "Nothing could be finer than to have him standing alongside you when your aim is to dump the bastard who'd had the gall to cheat on you."

"Yeah, Butch definitely has his uses."

"I seem to remember that he's pretty keen on you as well," Chelsey said. "Any chance of you giving him a go?"

Tamzin sighed heavily and took another sip from her drink. "I doubt it. He's going through a marriage breakup himself, so his head isn't really in the right place."

"That's a shame. Mind you, you know what they say about men built like The Rock, don't you?" Chelsey asked.

Tamzin rolled her eyes. "No, but I think I can guess. Go on, enlighten me."

"They lack size elsewhere on their anatomy."

The three of them laughed, and Tamzin shook her head.

"I won't tell him you said that and, furthermore, I have no intention of finding out whether that information is true or not."

"Go on, I dare you. You could regard it as research and share the results with us."

"Sod off. What type of girl do you take me for?" Tamzin bristled.

Chelsey chuckled. "One who is willing to go the extra mile for her friends."

The banter between them went back and forth for the next twenty minutes. They had known each other since their school days. Joined at the hip most of the time from the age of eleven when they started secondary school together. All of them terrified of what moving to a big school would entail. They'd had each other's backs ever since. Actually, the threesome had once been a group of four, but Denise had moved down south, to Devon, at the age of fourteen. Although, they were still in touch with her today, and she often visited them when she was able to get time off work.

During the evening, when the mood took them and the DJ played a hit that appealed to them, they strutted their stuff on the dance floor.

"The music is pretty naff tonight, isn't it?" Chelsey asked on her way back to the table after one such jig.

"It's not the best, is it?" Polly agreed. "Ahem, hunk alert." She thumbed over her shoulder at a table a few feet away.

Chelsey and Tamzin followed her gaze to where a group of five men were sitting, one or two of whom appeared to be taking an interest in them.

"Wow, now that's set my heart racing. Take your pick, girls, but the blond is mine," Tamzin gushed.

"You're unbelievable. Your bed isn't cold from the last one yet. Why don't you give the rest of us a chance first, mate?"

Chelsey eyed the bloke near the back, with the slight beard. Not that she was into hairy features, it was just that some men suited that kind of look, and he was definitely one of them.

"Which one is drawing your attention, Polly?"

"Not sure if any of them are, you know how fussy I am."

"Shit!" Chelsey hissed. "One of them is heading our way."

It was the fella Tamzin had earmarked as her own. He was slim and neatly turned out, as her mother would say.

"Hello, ladies. How are you doing?"

Chelsey and Polly took a metaphoric step back and allowed Tamzin to reply. She fluttered her eyelashes at him and turned on her usual charm, using her Marilyn Monroe voice to good effect. Chelsey groaned inwardly.

"Oh, hi. We're having a blast, aren't we, girls? I'm Tamzin by the way. Most of my friends, when they know me well enough, call me Tammy."

He perched on the seat beside her and placed his hand on her knee. "Well, Tammy, how about you and your friends join us for a few drinks?"

Tamzin smiled and then shot Chelsey and Polly a look. "What do you say, girls?"

"I reckon we're having a good enough time, just the three of us, aren't we?" Polly mumbled.

Chelsey was the only one who caught what she'd said over the din of the music. "Maybe another time. I thought we were supposed to be on a girls' night out. That usually means no men."

Tamzin glared at her as if to say, *speak for yourself. When an opportunity like this comes along, I ain't about to swerve it.* "Oh, really? Come on, girls, where's the harm in joining these lovely guys for a few drinks and maybe a dance or two? What's your name, hon?"

"I'm Oscar. Named after Oscar Wilde by my mum who is

an avid reader of literature dating back to the eighteen hundreds."

"That's right, the nineteenth century," Chelsey said. "And he was more known as a playwright," she added.

Oscar laughed. "Hey, I was only teasing. I have no idea if I was named after him or not, all I know is that the name has blighted my life and I prefer to be called Ozzy."

"You'll be telling us next that you were named after Ozzy Osborne." Tamzin chortled.

"I'll leave that up to you. I'll tell you one thing, I'm not as outrageous as that guy, which has to go in my favour, right?"

"Yep, I'm not keen on him or what he used to get up to in his earlier days. Could never see what Sharon Osborne saw in him, but they say love has a way of shining through adversity, don't they?"

"I bet she's just as wild as he is, that's why they're a match made in Heaven," Ozzy agreed. "So, what do you reckon, ladies, are you going to join us or not?"

Tamzin's pleading expression made it difficult for Chelsey and Polly to resist Oscar's charming proposal.

"Maybe one drink, see how we go, eh?" Chelsey said.

Smiling, Tamzin hooked her arm through Oscar's. "Lead the way, young man. We're all yours."

At first Polly and Chelsey felt uncomfortable in their new surroundings, but the more drink they consumed, the more they loosened up in the men's company. Chelsey watched Tamzin flirting with Oscar, dragging him on the dance floor periodically, when a slow number filled the room. A couple of the other men came on to them, appearing to be in competition as to who could whip out the corniest chat-up line. Karl's attempt was rather lacklustre and made Chelsey cringe. "Your eyes are like IKEA... I could get lost in them."

Chelsey sighed and shook her head, but that was mild compared to what Erik had in store for her. He leaned in and whispered in her ear, "Let's flip a coin... heads, I'm yours, and tails, you're mine."

"Give me a break," Chelsey groaned.

"I could do better, if you come back to mine." Erik grinned.

"You need your head read if you think a corny chat-up line is going to work on either of us."

He shrugged, unhitched his arm from her shoulder and moved away. In the meantime, Polly appeared to be getting on well with Karl, leaving Chelsey feeling like a spare piece of meat hanging at a cattle market, ready for the taking.

The next one on the list to try his hand was Ronan. He sidled up next to Chelsey and asked, "Do you want another drink?"

Picking up her half-filled cocktail glass, she smiled. "I think this one is going to last me a while, but thanks all the same."

"Fair enough. You must be tired, though."

She frowned. "Must I? How do you work that one out?"

He leaned closer and whispered the punchline in her ear, "Because you've been running through my mind all evening."

"Seriously, that's far worse than anything else I've heard tonight. Do any of these chat-up lines ever work?"

Aghast, he slapped a hand across his chest. "I'm appalled that you should think so badly of me. As if I'd used it many times before on unsuspecting victims."

She cocked an eyebrow. "Haven't you?"

A sheepish grin lit up his clean-shaven face. "Once or twice, that's all, though."

"Pray tell me, did it work?"

He screwed up his nose and sighed. "Negative."

"Perhaps that should tell you something, either give up or purchase a better book of chat-up lines."

"Okay, I'll take that on board. Thanks for the tip. Do you come here often…? Shit, I can't believe I asked you that."

Chelsey chuckled. "Neither can I."

"Well, do you?" Ronan prompted.

"We've only been once or twice. I've not noticed your group here before."

"This is our first time." He held up his hand and waved it from side to side. "Not sure it's worth the exorbitant entrance fee. I'd heard they had dropped the price in the last couple of months, but if they want to fill the place, they're going to need to rethink their prices for the future, wouldn't you agree?"

"Definitely. The first time we came we paid a tenner each on top of what we paid tonight, but after listening to the shite music they've played most of the evening, I can't see us coming back anytime soon."

"I'm glad we agree on something."

Oscar appeared beside them, his arm flung limply around Tamzin's shoulders. "We've decided to go back to Erik's place, haven't we Tamzin? Are you guys going to tag along?" He whispered something in Tamzin's ear and she giggled.

Chelsey's heart sank. She wasn't the type to go off with a group of men she'd met only an hour or so before. She held her tongue until Polly gave her response.

"Sounds good to me," Polly said. She nudged Chelsey in the back. "Come on, you know you want to. It's got to be better than hanging around this dive for the rest of the evening."

"You guys go. I'm going to call it a night."

"Coward," a male voice goaded her from behind.

She faced Erik who was standing beside Daniel, the only man who had remained silent so far. "I'm anything but. We've only just met you and we know nothing about you."

"And your point is?" Erik challenged.

"Come on, Chelsey, don't be a spoilsport," Polly whined, her eyes glassy from the mojitos she'd been downing all evening.

Chelsey held up her hands. "I'm not going to be the one to throw a spanner in the works but, ladies, I need to have a private chat with you first, alone."

She turned and walked towards the ladies' toilets on the next level, hoping that Polly and Tamzin would join her. It took them a while, but eventually that's exactly what her friends did.

"What's going on?" Tamzin asked, her arms folded. She leaned against one of the sinks in the plush bathroom.

"I might ask you two the same. This is so unlike you, guys. None of these blokes appeal to me in the slightest, and yet you're expecting me to go back to Erik's place, both of you paired up and me a sitting duck for them to come on to. That's not what I signed up for when I agreed to come out this evening, and it's wrong of you to think I'll roll over on this one."

"That's so unfair. I happen to like Oscar, he's got a great sense of humour and is really good-looking," Tamzin moaned.

"And I like Karl," Polly added.

Chelsey held her hands upside down and shrugged. "That settles it then, doesn't it?"

"No, it doesn't," Polly replied. "We all have to agree to going back to Erik's place or..."

"Or?" Chelsey asked. "I'll tell you what would be more appropriate."

"What's that?" Tamzin folded her arms tighter.

"If you two took down their numbers and agreed to meet up with them some other time, on a double date, if necessary. I think you're being grossly unreasonable, not to mention unfair, expecting me to tag along just because you ladies have hooked up with a couple of fellas you both like."

Tamzin's eyes flickered shut. She tutted then opened them again. "Why do we always have to do what you say?"

Gobsmacked by her friend's outburst, Chelsey took a step back. "It's always been a joint decision what we do, which is why I asked to speak with you privately. Please don't turn the tables on me, make me out to be the ogre here, not when we made a pact and have always stuck to it. Why should tonight be any different?"

"We're not making you out to be the ogre. Surely there are going to be times when plans get altered along the way. Maybe this is one of those times." Tamzin sighed.

"Hey, I don't think we should fall out about this, guys. Please don't do it," Polly pleaded, tears brimming.

Chelsey hated seeing her friends so upset, and yet on the flip side she detested that they were the ones not prepared to listen to her point of view. She heaved out a breath. Her arms flew out to the sides then smacked against her thighs. "Okay, you win. I'm clearly outnumbered here. I'll go along with you for an hour or so, only because the night is still young and I was intending on having a good time tonight, but don't expect me to sleep with any of the others."

"Hey, what are you saying? That we're going to part our legs for Karl and Oscar?" Polly asked, stunned.

"There's every chance that's going to happen, considering how much drink the boys have bought you this evening, already."

Polly and Tamzin glanced at each other and shrugged.

"I don't feel pissed," Polly admitted. "I still feel capable of making my own decisions."

"Good. Glad to hear it. But we all know that can change once you step out into the fresh air. You need to be prepared for that, hon."

"And I will be," Polly insisted. "So, are you giving us the green light to enjoy ourselves tonight?"

"Yes, with an added word of caution thrown in for good measure: don't let them do anything to you that goes against your principles."

"We won't, will we, Tammy?"

"No way."

They high-fived each other and carried out the necessary in the ladies' before rejoining the group of men, who were eagerly awaiting their decision.

Tamzin made herself spokesperson and announced, "It's a goer, gents, if the invite is still on the table?"

Oscar was the first to jump out of his seat. He picked Tammy up and spun her around before he planted a kiss on her lips. "Excellent news. You won't regret it, ladies." He whispered something extra in Tammy's ear, and she laughed raucously.

"Okay, let's get this show on the road," Erik said.

A couple of them chose to finish off their drinks while the others followed Erik out of the club and onto the main street. He flagged down two cabs, and they all piled into the back, four in each of the cars. Chelsey got separated from Polly and Tammy, which soured her mood considerably.

The three men she was travelling with all joked around her. Not once did they ask her to join in with the conversation, making her feel even more uncomfortable than she already felt about tagging along with her friends. Her focus remained outside, watching the different stragglers from the clubs and bars in the city centre making fools of themselves. *I'm glad I never let myself get into a state like that, an added bonus, in my opinion.*

"Penny for them?" Ronan nudged her out of her daydream.

"Just sitting here, watching the world go by." *Wishing I was out there instead of travelling with you lot, but hey, them's the breaks.*

"We'll show you a good time, the evening is still young yet, Chelsey."

She smiled. "Can't wait," she replied, sounding unconvincing to her own ears.

THE TAXIS DREW to a halt outside a double-fronted new-build on the edge of the city but in the opposite direction to the nightclub where they'd met. Chelsey knew this area fairly well, as another one of her friends, Maisie, had moved out this way with her fella a few months earlier.

Erik paid the driver. The other guys chipped in, but they refused to take any money off Chelsey, which suited her. It was going to cost her later to return home anyway.

He showed them into his house. The other guys were blasé about their surroundings, but Chelsey had a hard time disguising how much she admired Erik's taste in furnishings.

"This is stunning," she muttered as he swept past, relieving everyone of their coats and placing them on the chair in the large hallway.

"Thanks, feel free to have a wander. What do you all want to drink? I have a couple of bottles of prosecco chilling in the fridge."

"I can lend a hand, if you want," Chelsey offered.

Erik smiled and led the way into the state-of-the-art kitchen that took her breath away.

"You like it?" He beamed.

"I do, it's impressive. Have you been here long?"

"Not that long, a few months. I had a hand in the build, what you see here is all my design."

"It's amazing. You have a keen eye for detail."

"I like to think so. Both my parents are property developers, they gave me a few pointers here and there."

"And what do you do for a living?"

"I'm a boring IT consultant. The only upside to that is that it pays well. I work for a firm that only deals with prestigious clients in the area. It means I work more than forty hours a week which can be a pain in the arse at times."

"I suppose you have to take the rough with the smooth. I bet you get a couple of weeks off at Christmas, don't you?"

"I do, actually, three weeks. I generally take off on holiday around that time."

"Anywhere interesting?"

"The slopes, Switzerland usually. Again, it's what my parents used to get up to when I was growing up, and I've tended to continue with that tradition. Have you ever been?"

"No, to be honest, it's not something that has ever appealed to me. I don't possess great balancing skills, they're questionable at the best of times. I fear I'd never be able to stay upright on the slopes."

"Never say never, balance can be taught. Just like a lot of things in this life, having the correct mindset to begin with is sometimes all you need to get started."

"I'll have to take your word for that. Where are the glasses?"

"Top cupboard, over on the right there."

She opened the double cupboard and removed eight glasses. He joined her and popped the corks on the two bottles of Prosecco. He handed one to Chelsea and, between them, they filled the glasses and ferried them into the open-plan lounge. Erik then put on some decent music and, for the first time in the past few hours, Chelsea began to relax. The two couples started dancing, oblivious to those around them, but Chelsea was happy sitting, listening in to the snippets of conversations going on around her. About an hour later, she found herself struggling to keep her eyes open and ended up falling asleep on the couch.

Her eyes flickered open when she sensed someone moving close by. She was lying on the couch and covered with a blanket. With a muzzy head, Chelsey struggled to focus. Eventually, her vision cleared, and she saw Erik and Ronan both staring at her from their stools at the bar.

"Good morning, sleepyhead. You were well away there," Erik called over, his eyes twinkling with what she perceived as mischief.

She yawned and stretched her arms above her head. The blanket slipped and revealed that her top had been removed and she had slept in her bra. Mortified, she covered her modesty once more but not before she peeked under the blanket. There, she saw that not only had her top been removed but her trousers had as well. Her gaze latched on to Erik's.

He cocked an eyebrow and asked, "Something wrong?"

Not wishing to cause a scene until she'd got her thoughts in order, she shook her head. "No, everything is fine." She searched the floor to her left and discovered her clothes had been folded in a neat pile.

Polly and Karl entered the room, their arms wrapped around each other. Polly kissed him on the cheek and raced across to join Chelsey. "Hey, how did you get on?"

"I need to get out of here, now," Chelsey hissed.

"What's wrong? Didn't you have a good time?"

"No questions, not here. We need to leave. Where's Tammy?"

"I just saw her going into the bathroom. Is everything all right?"

"Keep your voice down. No, everything is far from okay. Go and fetch Tammy, tell her to get a move on."

Polly seemed perplexed by the request. "But why?"

"No questions," she repeated through clenched teeth.

Polly left the room. The three men appeared to be distracted, allowing Chelsey the time to gather her clothes and get dressed, her uneasiness notched up to another level when she felt stickiness between her legs. Polly and Tammy entered the room as Chelsey was folding up the blanket. She draped it over the back of the comfy corner couch, a huge question running through her mind: *what happened last night?*

"Morning," Tammy said, her usual bright, cheery self.

"Morning. Are you ready to go?" Chelsey picked up her bag and placed it over her shoulder.

"What? Can't we at least grab a coffee and a piece of toast first?" Tammy complained.

"No. I need to go, now."

Polly rolled her eyes at Tammy. "That's our breakfast spoilt then."

"I'm sorry," Chelsey murmured through clenched teeth. "I'll explain all when we leave. Now make your excuses, do what else you have to do, and I'll meet you at the front door." She slipped on her shoes and tore out of the room. In the hallway, she bumped into Daniel.

"Hello, lovely lady. In a hurry to leave, are we?"

"Yes, I have to be somewhere."

"Ah, a very busy person, eh?"

She swallowed down the bile rising in her throat. "Especially at the weekend. Life never stops for some of us."

Polly and Tammy finally appeared, putting an end to her awkward conversation with Daniel.

"We're off, see you around," Chelsey called over her shoulder. She opened the front door and left.

"How are we going to get home? Or haven't you thought that far ahead?" Tammy asked.

"We'll ring for a taxi. I needed to get out of that house."

The wind was relentless while they waited for the driver to pick them up. Luckily, it remained dry until they were settled in the back of the taxi.

"Right, are you going to tell us what's going on?" Tammy demanded.

"Sorry to spoil your fun and any thoughts you had of mooching around having a lazy breakfast."

"All right, calm down. Why are you being so sarcastic with us, Chelsey?"

"Because... something happened last night..."

Polly and Tammy shared a quizzical look.

"You're going to have to give us more than that," Polly said.

Chelsey eyed the driver in his rear-view mirror. He didn't appear to be listening in on their conversation.

She lowered her voice and said, "I woke up this morning half-dressed."

Tammy laughed. "Didn't we all?"

Chelsey seethed. "You had reason to be in that state, I didn't. When I fell asleep last night, I was fully clothed, and this morning..."

"No, that's unreal," Polly said, aghast. "What are you saying?"

"Oh, I don't know. There might be an innocent reason behind me waking up in my underwear, but at the moment, I'm struggling to think what it might be. Feel free to chip in with any bright ideas that may come your way."

"Jesus, why are you taking this out on us?" Tammy said, crossing her arms and huffing out a few impatient breaths.

"I'm not. All I'm telling you is the truth about what happened."

"And what did happen?" Polly pressed.

"Fuck, I don't know. You tell me. I'm at a loss to know how it happened, to me of all people."

The car fell silent, until Tammy finally whispered, "Are you saying someone did something to you?"

Chelsey shrugged. "I don't know. I wish I did but I have no recollection of what went on last night."

"Too much drink?" Polly asked.

"I didn't think I had, but it would appear to be the case. I still think I would've remembered getting undressed, though, don't you?"

Tammy sucked on her lip and tutted. "Yeah, I remember getting undressed last night and I think I had more to drink than you."

"It's not about who drank the most," Chelsey said. "This is about me not being able to remember something as significant as undressing the night before."

"I get times when I can't recall what I've said and done the day before, we all do, don't we?" Polly asked.

Chelsey glared at her. "Not me. Ever."

"So, what are you saying, Chelsey?"

She shrugged, infuriated with her friends and her lack of recall. "I don't know but I intend to find out."

CHAPTER 2

For the past three weeks, Chelsey had felt the need to distance herself from the others. Their lack of empathy for her plight was just too much for her to bear. Since that experience, she had kept herself to herself, only venturing out to work, never out at night for any alcohol-laced pleasure. Although, it meant her life had become miserable without her friends and the freedom to go out when she wanted to. Recently she woke up with a bad rash on her right side. Concerned, she decided to get it checked out by the doctor. He gave her antihistamines and a cream that didn't really make a lot of difference. Being consumed with itchy skin blighted her life and caused sleep-deprivation that turned out to be extremely hard for her to handle. It was impossible for her to function properly without the appropriate amount of sleep.

Anyway, with her skin not clearing up, she rang the surgery and managed to get an appointment with a different doctor who suggested they run some blood tests to see what was going on. He asked her a bunch of personal questions about her sex life that made her squirm in her seat due to her recent experience. Bloods were taken, and she was told to make another appointment to see the same doctor for the results.

She duly showed up for her appointment, her skin still sore and very itchy.

The doctor told her to sit down. He placed his forearms on his thighs and said, "I have your results and I'm sorry to have to tell you that you have HIV."

Chelsey's heart seemed to jump into her mouth. She struggled to find the appropriate words to respond to the devastating news.

"Are you all right, Miss Flores?"

Her head jutted forward. "Would you be after someone has just handed you a death sentence?"

He laughed.

"I'm so pleased you find it amusing, but then, it's not your life that's on the line here, is it?"

"I'm sorry. I didn't mean to laugh. It's not as bad as it used to be. Medication has come a long way since HIV was discovered."

"Glad to hear it. Umm… can you get it if you're not gay? Excuse my ignorance, I don't really know much about the topic, because I've never felt the need to research it."

"No, it's no longer considered to be a disease that only blights gay people's lives. In fact, it's far more prevalent in heterosexual people. It's more about how people have sex and the lives they lead."

"Can you be more specific? My mind is blown right now, I can't believe I'm hearing this."

"It can be drug related. Transmitted sexually through bodily fluids."

"Well, we can definitely discount the use of drugs, I've always refused to try them. I value my brain cells too much."

The doctor smiled. "That's it. Glad to see you're able to joke about it."

"I wasn't aware that I was. I think I'm still in shock. What's the next step? Is there a cure for it? Or is it a death sentence I have to deal with for the rest of my life?"

"We can discuss all of that in the future. I'll give you some leaflets for you to read at your leisure. Try not to believe everything you find on the internet. Any questions, don't hesitate to ask me. Let it sink in and come back next week when we can discuss the options available to you."

"Thanks, I think. How long have I got?"

He shook his head. "It is not a death sentence, you must get that out of your head. Yes, it is going to have a devastating effect on your life going forward, but with medication we can pave the way to a brighter future for you."

"Seriously? I always presumed there was no way back from it."

"It's a gross misconception. Read the leaflets, and we'll discuss things further. Umm... I feel it's my duty to tell you that you might want to inform anyone you've slept with recently, possibly in the last couple of months or so."

She gasped. "You think they've transmitted it to me? Would they have known?"

He shrugged. "Not necessarily. Let's face it, the only reason we know that you have it is because we ran the bloods because you developed the rash."

"What if they don't want to go to the doctor, what then?"

"They're morally obligated, but no one can force them to take a test. Saying that, you can buy HIV tests over the counter which will give you a result within thirty minutes, should they want to go down that route."

"I'll be sure to let them know." She waved the leaflet. "Thanks for the reading material, Doctor."

"Let's find you a slot on the system for next week. Ah,

here we are, virtually the same time, three-thirty on Thursday, how does that suit you?"

"Perfect." She opened up the calendar on her phone and noted down the appointment then stood. "Thank you, Doctor. It's been an eye-opener coming here today."

"Promise me you won't stress about it."

"I promise I won't. I'll see you next week."

In a daze, she left the surgery and decided to go for a walk along by the river to try and make sense of what the doctor had told her. It didn't work; in fact, having the time to think only made matters far worse. Unexpected tears emerged as she strolled towards her car. Chelsey sat there for a while and cried it out then drove back to the house, where she sat with a glass of brandy, to read the leaflets the doctor had given her.

Why me? How could this disgusting disease be affecting my life? What are people going to think of me? Why should it bother me what people think or say about me? It's not like I've been sleeping around for years, not like some girls I know. Fuck, where do I go from here?

After deliberating the same questions over and over for an hour, she finally picked up the phone and rang the two people she trusted most in this world, despite distancing herself from them for the past few weeks.

"Hey, you. I was thinking about you the other day. How are you diddling, my old mucker?" Tamzin mimicked something her father always said to his mates. Her voice was also warm and welcoming, no hint of anger or resentment in her tone, which pleased Chelsey.

"I've got some news. I need to see you and Polly ASAP. When can we meet up?"

"Anytime suits me, I'm not up to much."

"What about Oscar? Are you still seeing him?"

There was a slight pause before Tammy answered, "Off and on, nothing too heavy. Can you give me a hint what the meet-up is about?"

"I'd rather not say. Can you join me at The White Swan at the end of my road tonight, at around seven-thirty?"

"Sounds good to me. Are we eating out or should I have something at home?"

"I doubt if I'll feel like eating, so yes, eat before we get there."

"Sounds ominous. Are you sure you're okay, love? We've both missed you."

"I'm fine. See you later. If Polly has an issue with meeting us, I'll let you know. Is she still seeing Karl?"

"Yes, nothing concrete, a bit like me and Oscar, as and when we need to see them, if you get my drift?" Tammy laughed and hung up.

I hope you're using protection, for all your sakes. Chelsey dialled the second number. Polly sounded cautious at first and then relieved to hear her voice.

"God, I didn't think you were ever going to speak to either of us again, not after what happened. How have you been?"

"Surviving. Can you meet me tonight at The White Swan at the end of my road at seven-thirty? Tammy has already agreed to the venue and time, but if it doesn't suit you, we can scratch it and rethink."

"No, that sounds fine to me. Are we eating out?"

"Tammy asked the same. No, not this evening. I don't think I could stomach food today."

"Oh God! Why not? You've got to eat, Chels."

"I know, just not today. Don't worry about me, I'll be fine. See you later, I've got to fly now."

"Looking forward to it. Take care."

Chelsey jabbed the End Call button and sat there, staring at her mobile for what seemed like hours, wondering if she should call her mum to share the news. In the end, she decided to steer clear of any unwanted and unnecessary angst from her parents, until she'd had her discussion with Tammy and Polly.

She spent the next couple of hours forcing herself to unwind, but the more she tried, the more she became like a coiled spring. At six-thirty she ran a bath, hoping to soak away her concerns. She didn't bother washing her hair, aware of how long it would take her to dry and style it. Then she pulled on a clean pair of jeans and a jumper. Slipped on her new trainers and set off for the pub. During her five-minute walk from one end of the road to the other, her stomach succeeded in tying itself into knots of various sizes. Her breathing became laboured and hard to control as if she were climbing Mount Everest in a raging snow blizzard.

What the fuck is going on with me? Is this because of the HIV? Is this what I have to look forward to for the rest of my life? She shook the thought from her mind, not willing to entertain how debilitating the illness was likely to become over the coming months or even years, despite what she'd read on the leaflets to the contrary. She had learnt nothing, not really, and her mind was full of doom and gloom, and she couldn't see anything altering her stance on that anytime soon.

Glancing around the car park, she recognised her two friends' vehicles. She paused for a moment or two, not only to catch her breath but also to prepare for what lay ahead of her, fearing the conversation she was about to hold with her best friends was going to be far from easy. Chelsey sucked in several large breaths and let them out slowly. When she felt calm enough, she plucked up the courage to enter the door to the lounge bar of The White Swan, where they usually met up.

Polly was the first to hop off her stool at the bar to greet her. "Oh God, it's been so long since we've seen you. How have you been? Have you lost weight? Have you done something different to your hair?"

"Give the woman a chance to breathe, for fuck's sake." Tammy jumped down off her stool and tugged at Polly's arm, wanting a cuddle of her own. "It's great to see you. See, we left you alone as promised. Glad you saw the error of your ways and got in touch with us again. Any longer and I might have thought we'd seen the last of you."

Chelsey smiled and returned their hugs. "Once you hear what I have to say you might regret meeting me tonight. Shall we move to a table instead? It'll be more private."

Polly grabbed her drink from the bar and crossed the room to the table by the window, close to the wood burner.

"I'll get you a drink. What do you want, the usual?" Tammy asked.

"I'll just have an orange juice. I need to keep a clear head this evening."

"Fair enough. I'll get it in and join you in a mo."

Chelsey's eye was drawn to the fire blazing to her right. It was comforting and warmed her aching bones. She wondered if the chill running through her was to do with the weather or if it was more to do with the task that lay ahead of her.

Polly patted the bench seat beside her. "Here, sit next to me."

"I'd rather sit here. I'll let Tammy have that seat, that way it'll be easy to chat with both of you."

Polly shrugged and seemed offended to be turned down. *She'll get over it.* Tammy joined them moments later with their drinks. She slid Chelsey's across the table to her and sat next to Polly.

"What's up?" Tammy was the first to ask.

Suddenly, Chelsey's mouth dried up. She sipped at her drink and cleared her throat. "I have news for you that just can't wait. I wanted to tell you in person, rather than over the phone."

"Sounds worrying. Can you get on with it? You're scaring the crap out of me now."

Chelsey gave her friends a half-smile and clutched her hands together on the table in front of her. The aim was to prevent them from shaking.

"Come on, Chels, you're worrying me now. What's going on?" Tammy asked. She took a sip from her glass of white wine.

"This is so hard for me to say, please be patient with me."

"Of course, that goes without saying. In your own time, love," Polly assured her. She placed a hand over Chelsey's. "Do you want to talk about something else instead and we'll come back to the issue that is causing you angst? It's no problem."

"No, just give me a couple of minutes. Wait, maybe you're right. Why don't you tell me what you've been up to during our break apart?"

"I'll go first. I just got a promotion at the gym. I'm going to become the lead personal fitness expert for the day shift down there."

"That's amazing, something that has been on the cards for months for you. I'm thrilled, Tammy. When is that going to happen?"

"At the beginning of next month. It's about time, I've been overlooked for that position for years."

"Brilliant news. What about you, Polly?"

"No promotion for me. Just the same old routine, filling the shelves and making dozens of egg mayo sandwiches down at the baker's."

"Never mind, I'm sure they appreciate your work all the same."

"Nope, I don't think the owners have ever uttered any kind of praise, not from what I can remember."

Chelsey smiled. "It's their loss. Maybe they're not the type to show their gratitude."

"You can say that again. I can't recall the last time I had any form of bonus or pay rise from them either. I've been working there for eight years now."

"Would it be worth taking them to one side and having a word?" Tammy suggested.

"Have you met them? Nope, as long as the shops take enough to keep their two Merces on the road, I'm sure that's all they care about."

"Some people need a lesson in how to treat their staff properly," Chelsey chipped in.

"And some," Polly agreed.

The three of them took a sip from their drinks, and then Chelsey plucked up enough courage to reveal her distressing news.

"I want to thank you both for agreeing to meet me here this evening, especially after the way things ended between us. I regret walking away from our friendship but felt my hands were tied."

"We're going over old ground. You had your reasons for ditching us, let's not rake over all that again. What's changed?" Tammy asked, no sign of a smile on her face.

"Quite a lot. Umm... I've not been feeling too great lately and decided to make an appointment to see the doctor." She watched Polly and Tammy share a concerned glance.

"Oh God, you haven't got cancer, have you?"

"No, nothing like that. Well, maybe it is... oh God, I don't know how to put this." She peered over her shoulder to see if anyone nearby was listening to their conversation, despite her keeping her voice to a bare minimum. Feeling safe in the knowledge they couldn't be overheard, she ploughed on. "I went last week, and the doctor carried out some blood tests. I was told to go back today for the results."

"And? Christ, it's like having a painful tooth extracted…" Tammy complained. She sat back and folded her arms, her patience dwindling fast.

"Bugger, you're not preggers, are you?" Polly whispered conspiratorially.

Chelsey smiled. "No, nothing as clear cut as that."

"What's that supposed to mean? Get on with it, Chels, before I lose the bloody will to live."

Chelsey slapped a hand over her mouth, closed her eyes and shook her head. The words failed to materialise, and her mind was like a vortex, swirling in the atmosphere. It was okay knowing and dealing with what was going on with her, but bloody hell, it was a different thing entirely revealing what was going on with her body to the two people she considered to be her best friends.

"Chels, please, you can trust us, you know that, don't you?" Polly said. She gathered Chelsey's hand in her own and clung on tight.

The gesture went a long way towards comforting her. "I know I can trust you, it's not that. I'm simply struggling to find the right words to tell you. Give me a second or two." With her free hand, she picked up her glass and took another long swig of her drink. The delay gave her enough time to gather her thoughts again. She blew out the breath she'd been holding in and tried a second time. "Right, well, the results came back and…" Again, her lungs emptied quickly, and she found herself gasping for breath.

"My God, what the hell is wrong with you?" Tammy asked. She sidled up closer to Chelsey.

Tears pricked and threatened to fall. "I had it all planned out, how and what I wanted to say, but now the time is here, I'm struggling to get the damn words out."

"Just say it," Polly pleaded. "Tell us and we'll thrash it out between us. Come up with a solution to your problem, the way we always have, together."

Chelsey gave her friend a faint smile. "The thing is, I don't see an easy fix to this one, hon."

"Let us be the judge of that," Tammy urged. "Come on, out with it."

Chelsey gulped. She needed to get this out in the open now, even if God struck her down. *Hasn't He done that already, handing me this death sentence? Despite the doctor telling me it isn't, I'm always going to think of it that way. I'm bound to.* "Oh, shit. How do I put this into words? I'm not good at dealing with things of this magnitude. Up until now, life has been relatively simple for me, but I have to say, the news I received today from the doctor has rocked my world, and no, this isn't me being overdramatic, I promise."

Polly squeezed her hand. "Just tell us. It doesn't matter if the words come out wrong, we'll deal with that afterwards. You're worrying us, sweetie."

"I'm sorry, that wasn't my intention." Chelsey peeked over her shoulder again and then leaned in to whisper, "The doctor told me today that I have HIV."

She sat back and waited for the news to sink in. Polly was the first to react. She slapped her hands on either side of her face, and her mouth gaped open, showing off two of her most recent fillings.

"Are you sure? Shouldn't you get a second opinion for something like that?" Tammy asked, her voice hushed, pitched at barely above a whisper.

"Why prolong the agony? The proof was there in my blood test for all to see."

Polly started crying, and Chelsey's heart went out to her.

"I'm so sorry. How long have you got?"

Chelsey shrugged. "According to the doctor it's not as bad as it once used to be and there are certain medications I can take to keep the symptoms at bay. I have to go back and see him next week."

"I'll come with you," Tammy said, her voice raised.

"No, you won't. This is my problem; I can deal with it myself."

"Shit, have you told your parents?" Polly asked.

"Not yet. How the frigging hell I'm going to do that is another mighty weight sitting on my shoulders."

Tammy's hand swept over her face, and she stared at the floor beside her for a while. "I'm sorry, I don't know what to say, Chels. You know how unusual that is for me, I've usually got an opinion on any discussion that crops up, but not this time. That might change once the news sinks in. I'm gutted this has happened to you. Is there any way of the doctors knowing how long you've had this? Where you got it from?"

"Well, considering I haven't slept with anyone for two years, not since that arsehole John dumped me…"

Tammy placed her elbows on her knees and covered her head with her hands. "What are you saying?"

"I think you know as well as I do what this means, Tammy."

"Hey, what am I missing here?" Polly asked, her gaze flicking between them.

Chelsey left it for Tammy to fill her in.

"Well, you know what happened a few weeks ago, the night we met up with the group of men and ended up going back to Erik's gaff."

It was Polly's turn to gasp. "No way. This can't be happening."

"Oh, it's happening all right, I can assure you." Chelsey lifted her jumper to reveal the extent of her rash.

"Holy shit! You're kidding me. How long have you had that?"

"Long enough. This is the reason I went to the doctor in the first place. I never dreamt this would be the bloody outcome."

Polly whispered several expletives. "This is unbelievable. I'm so sorry you're having to contend with this."

Chelsey shrugged. "I suppose I'll get used to it. Right now, I'm really angry, not only that one of those fuckers took advantage of me that night but also because they didn't use any protection and have now ruined my life forever."

"What are you going to do about it?" Tammy asked.

"I'm not sure. I suppose I wanted to run it past you guys first, see what you make of the situation and then go from there. Has anyone said anything? Admitted to you that things went too far that night? You're still in touch with them, aren't you? Surely, they must have said something."

Polly and Tammy looked at each other and shrugged.

"I don't think any one of them has said a word, not to us anyway. Do you want us to ask them?" Tammy asked.

"No. I need to think things through, see which way I want to play this. I'm open to suggestions, though, if you want to throw anything into the ring."

Tammy puffed out her cheeks. "I'm lost for words and totally out of ideas right now."

"Me, too," Polly added. "It's a lot to take in, Chelsey, we're going to have to come to terms with it all before we can hatch a plan to rectify things."

Chelsey nodded. "You can imagine how I felt when the doctor gave me the results earlier. He handed me some leaflets, told me to read them, but that just made matters ten times worse."

"I'm so sorry you're having to deal with this shit, Chels. I wouldn't wish this type of news on my worst enemy," Tammy said. "I'm sure, if we put our heads together, we'll be able to come up with a solution. I mean, not to your main problem but to the issue regarding who the culprit is. Can you leave it with us for a few days?"

"Sounds good to me. I have to return to the doc's on Thursday to have further discussions with him."

"Good, I'm sure he'll be able to offer you some sound advice. Have you asked Google? About what symptoms to expect and what the prognosis is likely to be?"

"Not yet, I've been avoiding it. The doctor told me not to believe everything I read on the internet."

"Which is all well and good, and mostly I agree with him, but it can be a great source of information. You just need to pick and choose carefully."

"And how will I know what information is right and wrong?" Chelsey said, challenging Tammy's suggestion.

She hitched up a shoulder and blew out a breath. "How the heck should I know? I don't even know anyone I can ask, not knowing anyone who has dealt with this shit."

"Exactly, I'm in the same boat, which is why I came running to you guys for help."

"No pressure there then," Polly said.

Chelsey covered her face with her hands. "It's all such a mess. If only we hadn't agreed to go back with those bastards that night… I wouldn't be dealing with this traumatic dilemma now."

"And that's our fault, is it?" Tammy asked, her eyes narrowing slightly.

"Did I say that?" Chelsey bit back.

"Ladies, falling out about this isn't going to remedy the situation, is it?" Polly asked.

Chelsey mumbled an apology. "I'm confused, bewildered and unable to think straight. How long is that likely to last?"

"Your guess is as good as ours," Tammy admitted. "We'll be by your side every step of the way. We can both have a word with our respective fellas, see what they have to say about the matter."

"No," Chelsey shouted. She glanced over her shoulder at the table behind and smiled at the customers. "Sorry, I didn't mean to snap. You can't tell them, not the truth."

"As if we would," Tammy assured her. "Leave it with us, we'll get to the bottom of this, I promise. Won't we, Polly?"

"Sure, if that's what you think, Tammy. In the meantime, we'll put our heads together and come up with a plan to deal with the issue."

"I'm concerned that the person responsible will go on to rape someone else and infect them."

"It doesn't bear thinking about, does it?" Tammy agreed.

Chelsey shook her head. "Nope. What a bloody mess."

The conversation dried up, leaving the three of them fidgeting in their seats. Chelsey began to wonder if she'd done the right thing, coming here, telling the others what the doctor had said. After all, they were both still involved with two of the men. What if the rapist turned out to be one of them? It seemed unlikely, considering their partners were probably with them all night, but who knew if that was the case or not?

"What are you thinking, Chels?" Tammy asked after a while.

"I'm not, not really. The same crippling scenario keeps running through my mind that I'm having trouble shifting."

"Are you going to tell us what that is?"

"I keep thinking about the impact this disease is going to have on me every single day of my life, and most of all, what my parents are going to think of me when I finally reveal the truth. I feel totally ashamed about that."

It was Tammy's turn to reach for her hand. "Well, don't. None of this is your fault. We're going to support you throughout, aren't we, Polly?"

"I should say so. The Three Amigos, through thick and thin, we promised to always be by each other's side."

"And yet, the last few weeks, when I walked away from you guys, tells a different story, doesn't it?"

"Nonsense, you had a right to be upset, angry, call it what you will about that predicament and, as it has turned out, your instinct has been proved right," Tammy said.

"So, what are we going to do about it?" Chelsey asked. She sat upright as a cruel image popped into her mind.

"Question the men, one by one. Maybe getting them alone will make them open up and admit they were in the wrong," Tammy suggested. "Hey, what are you thinking, Chels? I know when you're away with the fairies, dreaming up a plan."

She smiled. "You really don't want to know."

"You're wrong, we do. Come on, spill!"

Chelsey took her time to sort out the words flying around in her head and put them in some kind of order.

"Come on, we're eager to hear it." Polly nudged her.

Another quick glance over her shoulder, and then Chelsey whispered, "What if we force the information out of them?"

Tammy and Polly both sat back and stared at her before Tammy asked, "What are you saying?"

Polly's mouth dropped open, and she shook her head. "No, you're talking about doing something illegal, aren't you?"

"Are you?" Tammy demanded.

"Possibly. What if we pick up each of the men, take them

somewhere remote and beat the shit out of them, you know, to force the truth out of them?"

"Oh shit, you can't be serious?" Polly asked, her gaze darting between them.

"I would say that she's deadly serious," Tammy added.

Chelsey blew out a breath and then sipped at her drink. "It's just something that sprang to mind. Of course, the idea will need tweaking before we can put anything into action."

"I say we do it," Tammy said. "What have we got to lose?"

Polly looked disgusted by the proposal. "You're kidding me?"

Chelsey smiled. "Like I said, it'll need tweaking. But the more I think about it, the more inclined I am to think this is the way to go. All we need to do now is figure out where to take the men once we've abducted them."

"Holy crap. You really are serious about this," Polly muttered.

"I think she might be on to something," Tammy agreed. "I'm in, if you guys are?"

Polly raised her hands and shook her head. "Whoa, just a minute, this idea is growing so fast even Usain Bolt wouldn't be able to keep up with it. It's not feasible to consider. You can't just pluck an idea out of the air and expect us to all agree with it."

"What's the alternative?" Tammy challenged. "That we let the fuckers get away with it? What if the person knew he had HIV and deliberately targeted Chelsey, knowing that she would be alone on the couch all night?"

"That's a sick suggestion." Polly chewed on her ruby-red lips.

"It possibly is, but who's to say it's not the truth? What do you reckon, Chels?"

"My honest opinion is that I was probably drugged that night, incapacitated for a reason. Yes, it's all making sense now. One of those guys, maybe more than one, spiked my drink with the intention of raping me when I was out cold. The fact the house was full of his friends was an extra buzz to the process." The more she thought about it, the more her idea became a possible reality.

"I can't believe what I'm hearing. You guys need to take a step back and consider what you're saying," Polly added as a word of caution.

"Hey, I don't think there's any harm in questioning the men," Tammy said, defending Chelsey's idea and the way it was evolving. "Hang on, didn't you say that you were looking after a friend's house while they were away in Australia?"

Polly gasped and waved her hands. "My God, don't even go there. Neil would string me up if he heard about this."

Chelsey nodded and smiled. "How is he going to hear if you don't tell him?" She sensed they were getting close to being on the same page as the idea steamrolled into a plausible concept.

"I need to check it out. He didn't tell me, but what if he's rigged the house up with security cameras and is keeping an eye on it remotely?"

"He'd be a fool not to nowadays. Burglaries are at an all-time high. Let's just say that I wouldn't take off to the other side of the world for six months and leave my house empty," Tammy said.

Polly bristled in her seat and retorted, "They haven't, they've entrusted me with a key to keep a close eye on it, and that's what I intend to do."

"The last thing I want to do is put you in an awkward position, Polly, but it does seem to be a good solution to our problem," Chelsey said.

"What the fuck? I can't believe I'm hearing this. It's all right to think that when the onus isn't sitting on your shoulders. What would you do if you found yourself in my position?"

"The right thing," Chelsey shot back.

"That's easy for you to say, it's my head that is on the chopping block, not yours."

Tammy raised her hands between them and said, "Ladies, let's simmer down before we start tearing chunks out of each other."

"God, how did we get here?" Polly said. She covered her head with her hands.

Chelsey suddenly felt guilty for making her friend suffer. "I'm sorry, love. It was wrong of us to put you in such a position. Forget we mentioned it."

"I wouldn't be so keen to dismiss the idea if I were you," Tammy added.

Again, the three of them fell silent as they contemplated what had been said.

Eventually, it was Polly who broke the silence. "All right, I'll do it. On one proviso."

"What's that?" Chelsey asked.

"That you help me clean the place up and that we leave it as we find it."

"Of course, that goes without saying, Polly. You have our word, doesn't she, Tammy?"

"Absolutely. Has anyone got a piece of paper and a pen?" Tammy asked.

Both Chelsey and Polly shook their heads, so Tammy left her seat and approached the bar. She returned carrying a notebook the barman had given her.

"Right, let's see what ideas we can come up with."

Polly and Chelsey smiled.

"Ever the organised one." Chelsey chuckled.

They spent the next half an hour batting ideas around while Tammy jotted things down.

"So, the location is sorted. How are we going to pick the guys up?"

"I assume we're going to need a van of sorts," Chelsey admitted.

"I can have a word with my brother, he's a mechanic," Tammy suggested.

"That's great. What about the men? Does anyone know where the others either live or work?" Chelsey asked. She fiddled with her glass on the coaster.

"Polly and I can get the relevant information out of Karl and Oscar, can't we?"

Polly's mouth twisted as she deliberated the question. "I suppose so. No harm in discreetly questioning them, is there?"

"The only thing we need to sort out now is when we should put our plan into action."

"If it was up to me, I would say sooner rather than later," Chelsey said. "My greatest worry is if this son of a bitch goes out on the pull and infects someone else. See, I'm not really being selfish about this, it's the concern for others that is driving me on."

"We know that and we're going to do all we can to support you, isn't that right, Polly?"

"We've already come to that conclusion. Are we done here now?"

"Do you have somewhere you need to be?" Chelsey asked, surprised.

"Yes, Karl and I are supposed to be meeting up tonight."

"Sorry, I thought you told me you were free this evening," Chelsey said. "Of course, you shoot off, we'll catch up with you again soon."

"And don't forget to pump him for information during the course of the evening, if the opportunity arises," Tammy said.

"I won't." Polly quickly kissed them on the cheek and dashed out of the pub.

Chelsey stared at the door, long after Polly had exited the bar. "Do you think we can trust her?"

"I bloody well hope so. Maybe we'll need to monitor the situation carefully. You know Polly, most of the time she's in a world of her own and does things without thinking. I believe we've drilled it into her how important this task is."

"I hope you're right. If she lets the cat out of the bag, we're going to find ourselves up shit creek, aren't we? Especially if she's supplying the location."

"We'll have to see about that. I have a feeling she'll come up with an excuse for us not to use it. Maybe we should consider another place we can use instead, just to be on the safe side."

"I'll get my thinking cap on when I get home. I'm so glad I have you guys on my side."

"Where else would we be? I'm gutted you're going through this, Chels, but we'll make sure we're standing alongside you every step of the way."

"You're amazing. I'd be lost without you guys. My biggest regret is that we went back to Erik's house that night, but I couldn't stand in the way of what you and Polly wanted."

"Maybe you should have put your foot down firmer and forced us to listen to you, then you wouldn't be in the mess you're in today. I'll always feel guilty that you felt obligated to tag along with us that night, especially when this is the outcome. But we'll get to the bottom of this and make the bastard suffer for what he's putting you through. Promise me one thing."

Chelsey tilted her head. "What's that?"

"That we'll never fall out about this."

Chelsey reached for Tammy's hands and squeezed them.

"You have my word. I've really missed you guys for the last few weeks."

"I know, I feel the same. I'm glad you plucked up the courage to ring us. A problem shared and all that. I'll keep making notes and try to source another location. Shall we agree to meet up again soon? When everything is set in stone, then we can decide when to put things into action."

"Sounds good to me. What about at the weekend, either Saturday afternoon or Sunday evening? I'm off to my parents' for Sunday lunch this week."

"Sunday evening would suit me. I'll text Polly, see if that's okay with her. Do you want another drink?"

"No, I think I'll head home now. I still have a lot of thinking to do about how I'm going to break the news to my parents or even if I'm going to go down that route."

"If you'll take some advice from me, I wouldn't say anything, not yet. Not until you really need to tell them. There's still a nasty stigma attached to the disease."

"I know, but if it is going to cause health issues for me further down the line, shouldn't I prepare them for the inevitable?"

Tammy rolled her sparkling brown eyes. "You really have an awful dilemma on your hands, don't you? I'm sorry, I don't have all the answers for you, not right now, but hopefully that will change soon."

They finished their drinks and left the pub. Outside, the wind had got up, and Chelsey tugged her coat collar up around her ears.

"Where's your car?" Tammy asked.

"I walked. Don't worry about me, I needed to clear my head a bit before I met up with you and Polly. I'll see you Sunday evening." Chelsey embraced Tammy in a suffocating hug.

"You know where I am if you need someone to talk to."

"I know, and for that I'm grateful. I'll be fine, once I've successfully managed to get my head around everything. At least I feel more positive about it all, now that I've spoken with you and Polly."

"Good, I'm glad to hear it. We'll see you through this and get the answers that you need. I'm going to give Oscar a call when I get home. Actually, I might visit him instead, it'll be easier to start the conversation going about the others."

"Makes sense to me. Let me know how you get on."

They parted, and Chelsey set off on a slow wander back to the house, her mind churning up a storm en route. Vivid images of what she'd like to do to the men once they were in the same room with her played out with every step she took.

Once home, she made herself a cup of coffee and snuggled up on the couch with Sooty, her cat. "Are we about to do the right thing, sweetie? Will you forgive me? Will I be able to forgive myself?"

Sooty curled up in her lap, purring as if she didn't have a care in the world. Chelsey glanced sideways and picked up the notebook on the side table next to her and began jotting down notes of her own, which she could compare to the ones Tammy was going to make when she got home.

Exhausted, she tumbled into bed an hour later but resisted the temptation to fall asleep, aware of what would consume her during the night. She'd had several nightmares since the horrendous experience at Erik's house which had left her wondering if he knew what had gone on that night. Numerous questions and scenarios had filled her mind over the last few weeks, since she'd been raped, and now, she realised, that because she had been diagnosed with HIV, those nightmares were about to become so much worse.

She switched off the light and pulled Sooty closer. Her purring aided her attempt to drift off to sleep. However, two hours later she was wide awake and sitting up in bed, fighting to keep the monsters out of her head.

ON SUNDAY EVENING, she decided to walk to the pub again, despite it spitting with rain. Polly and Tammy were already there and greeted her warmly with a hug and a kiss on the cheek.

"How are you both?"

"I'm okay. The news you gave us the other day has been at the forefront of my mind, though," Polly admitted.

"Mine, too," Tammy added. "Still, with the notes I've made and the plans I've already put into action, I think we'll be able to right the wrongs that happened that night."

Chelsey removed her notebook from her handbag and placed it beside the one sitting in front of Tammy. "I made a few notes, too."

"Excellent. Let's get you a drink and then find a quiet corner where we can chat. What do you want?" Tammy said.

"I'll have a glass of Chardonnay, thanks," Polly replied, smiling nervously.

Polly's head dipped, which hadn't gone unnoticed by Chelsey.

"How are you, Polly?"

"I'm fine and dandy, just like I always have been."

"And your date with Karl the other night? How did that go?"

"If you're asking if I pumped him for answers, then yes, but he wasn't as forthcoming as I would have liked him to have been."

"Oh, why's that?" Chelsey asked. She carried her drink to the far side of the bar and tucked herself into the corner on the benched seat.

Polly didn't answer the question, she squeezed in beside her, and Tammy sat opposite them on the single chair.

"I don't think we'll be overheard here, ladies."

Tammy flipped open the two notebooks and compared them. When she glanced up at Chelsey, her eyes widened. "Holy crap, my notes are mild in comparison to what you've got here. Are you sure about this, Chels?"

"Ouch, not the words I expected to hear. Have I gone OTT?"

Tammy chuckled and cleared her throat. "Possibly a tad."

"What's she written?" Polly finally asked.

She held out her hands for the notebooks, and Tammy placed her notes in the right and Chelsey's in the left.

"That's mine, and this one is Chelsey's, not that you'll be in any doubt when you read them."

"Heck! I'm not sure I want to read them now."

"Read them through your fingers if it will help," Tammy quipped.

Chelsey watched with interest as Polly first read the notes in Tammy's book before she moved on to what Chelsey had jotted down. Polly cringed when she slowly raised her head to look at her. "Bloody hell! We can't get away with this, can we?"

"There's no reason why we shouldn't. It's all about getting the truth out of them. We'll make them aware of the consequences from the outset, putting the ball firmly in their court. The choice will be down to them. Either they do the right thing or…" Chelsey grinned and ran a finger across her throat.

"How has it come to this? We're not thugs, and yet here we are, revelling in what atrocities we're about to inflict on these men," Polly muttered. "Nothing about this feels right to me."

Tammy placed a hand on Polly's thigh. "Either you're with us or you can choose to bow out now. Which is it?"

Polly's gaze darted between them, and she sighed. "No, I'm with you, even though it goes against the grain."

"I'll let you in on a secret, Polly. At first, I had severe apprehensions about this until I started adding to the list. Maybe you should give it a go. Think up some kind of punishment for these guys, it'll make you feel more involved."

"Christ, looking over the notes you two have made already, I couldn't possibly come up with anything as devious as you guys. I think you're both on a different level to me."

Chelsey and Tammy laughed.

"Nonsense," Chelsey said. "You don't know until you give it a try. Why don't you take the notes home with you tonight, read them through thoroughly, and we'll meet up again tomorrow to discuss everything? It can't be out in the open like this, though."

"I think that's unnecessary. I can tell you now, I won't be able to add anything, except one minor detail that I believe you might have forgotten about."

Chelsey frowned. "Go on, what's that?"

"How are you going to subdue the men? We won't have the strength to overcome them, will we?"

Chelsey rubbed at her chin and thought for a second or two then clicked her fingers. "What about that friend of yours who works in the care home? Do you think she'll be able to get her hands on a sedative we can use?"

"Jesus, and how do you propose I ask her? I can't come out and tell her the truth, can I?"

"No, but perhaps you can think about an excuse. Say your mum's cat is having trouble sleeping and keeping your mum awake at night, does she have anything you can use to sedate her."

"Oh, right, you make it sound so bloody simple. You're effectively asking me to ask her to put her job on the line for my mum's pussy."

Tammy tittered, and Polly glared at her.

"I'm glad you think it's funny. I'm appalled you could even put me in such a position."

"Okay, keep it down," Chelsey hissed. "We'll have a rethink and come up with a way to sedate them without getting your friend involved, how's that?"

"Good, it's bad enough that we're doing this in the first place without getting anyone else involved in our cruel plans," Polly replied. Her head sank.

Tammy and Chelsey shared yet another concerned glance, not for the first time.

"Are you in or out, Polly?" Tammy asked.

Polly remained quiet for the next few seconds and then eventually nodded. "I don't see that I have a lot of options left open to me. We've always been there for each other, why should this time be any different?"

"So, do you want to take the books home with you and add to them?" Tammy asked.

"No, I'll leave all the details up to you two to sort out and have a think about how we can sedate the men."

Chelsey thought some more. "Is it easy to buy Rohypnol over the internet?"

"Heck, it's not something I've ever thought of searching for before. I suppose everything is available, if you want it," Tammy replied. "I'll do some digging and get back to you. It could be the answer to our problem."

Chelsey nodded. "I think we're set to go then, ladies. All we need to do now is arrange a time that suits all of us for things to happen."

Tammy shrugged. "Any time suits me. The sooner the

better in my opinion. Our main aim is to get this bastard off the streets before he can infect someone else, right?"

"Yes. Okay, what if we start at the end of the week? How are your schedules looking for the week ahead? Polly?"

"Same as usual. Sounds good to me."

"Mine never alters," Tammy said.

"Ditto for me, too," Chelsey said. "Okay, let me have a think about it overnight. Tammy, you do the necessary research on the Rohypnol, and we should be good to go once we've got that to hand."

The girls paused to take a sip of their drinks. Polly's gaze drifted to the bar.

"Are you all right, Polly?" Chelsey asked, concerned for her friend.

"I think so. I'll tell you when this nightmare is over. I do wish you would get a second opinion about your health before we get down to the nasty business of punishing these men."

"I will. But if the blood tests are showing that I have it, it'll only be delaying the inevitable, won't it?"

Polly hitched up her shoulder. "Can you buy a test over the counter?"

"Hey, that's a brilliant idea. We could get a handful of them for the task ahead of us," Tammy agreed.

"Yes, that's a great idea. We could kidnap each of the men and force them to take the test. Pin them down and take the swabs, if necessary," Chelsey said, her thoughts spinning off in several directions. *I can buy them with my credit card.*

Tammy sat upright in her seat. "I've had a thought; I can ask my brother about the Rohypnol. A few years back, he and his friends used to like to experiment with a chemistry set one of his mates bought off the internet. I'll see if he can knock us up a crude form of it."

"Sounds bloody dangerous to me," Polly said.

Chelsey waved her hand. "It's still involving someone else. Can you trust your brother, Tammy?"

"Hey, he's above board. If I tell him what's happened, he'd be the first in line behind us with a bloody solution. That reminds me, he's given us the all-clear to use a van that he's recently had to take off the road."

Chelsey inclined her head. "Taken off the road? Can I ask why?"

"Because it would have cost too much to have repaired it, and the bloke didn't have the funds. But when the bloke agreed to hand it over, Simon sourced the parts from a scrapyard and repaired it. He's added it to his fleet now but only intends to use it for emergencies."

"Sounds great to me." Chelsey smiled. "Looks like everything is coming together."

"Can I just add a word of caution to the mix about involving your brother in all of this?" Polly said after a moment's pause.

Tammy waved away her apprehensions. "He's fine. He's got the gift of the gab, he'll work around it, if the need arises."

Polly shrugged. "If you say so. Does anyone else want another drink?"

"Go on then, you've twisted my arm," Tammy said.

Chelsey offered up her empty glass. "Same again for me. Do you want some money?"

"No, I've got these. I'll be right back."

As soon as Polly was out of earshot, Tammy leaned in and whispered, "What do you think about her?"

"Hard to say, isn't it? One minute I think she's up for it, and the next it sounds like she's digging her heels in. Who's to say how she's going to react on the day? Hopefully, her adrenaline will kick in and do us all a favour."

Tammy laughed. "Fingers crossed. I bet she turns out to be worse than us at dishing out the punishment."

Chelsey had her doubts about whether that would be the case or not, given the hatred for the men running through her since her diagnosis had been confirmed.

Polly returned with her hands full and set the glasses on the table. "Here you go, ladies. I'd like to propose a toast."

The other girls picked up their drinks in readiness.

"To righting the wrongs of that drunken night."

"Hear, hear," Tammy and Chelsey said in unison.

CHAPTER 3

Monday

"Morning, folks. How are we all today?" DI Sara Ramsey drifted into the incident room as if she didn't have a care in the world, which couldn't have been further from the truth. Today was the day her husband, Mark, was due to have an operation to remove one of his testicles. She had kissed him goodbye, asked for the umpteenth time that morning if he was sure he didn't want her to go with him, and he'd hugged her tightly and sent her on her way.

It had come as a shock when he'd revealed the truth about his testicular cancer around six weeks ago. She was furious the hospital seemed to be dragging their feet about getting his treatment started. The same old excuses had arisen about certain sections of the hospital being on strike, one after the other. In Sara's opinion, people's health should come before all that shit, but she had been wary about sharing her views publicly over the last couple of weeks.

The oncologist was hopeful that Mark's cancer was minor enough that he would be clear after the operation. Sara, who was usually an optimist, was hopeful he was right, but there still remained a niggling doubt in her gut whether Mark would soon be cancer-free or not after his operation.

The team were aware of what was going on at home but were careful to avoid the subject. Sara felt it wouldn't be right to keep them in the dark, aware that her mood and work would probably be affected by Mark's surgery plight.

All the team members wished her well, and she made herself a coffee, noting that Carla was the only one who was missing.

"Send Carla in when she arrives, if you would?"

She tackled her emails and the remains of yesterday's post, anything to keep her mind occupied. Carla entered the room five minutes later. She had a box of chocolates in one hand and a mug of coffee in the other.

"What in God's name are they for?" Sara accepted the gift.

"Just a little something to say we're all thinking of you both. They're from all the team, not just me. We had a whip-round, yeah, abysmal, isn't it? Shows how much we think of you."

Sara couldn't help but laugh. "Gee, I'm glad you guys think that much of me. No, seriously, you shouldn't have. He'll be fine, we both will."

"It's just a simple token to say we're thinking about you both at this difficult time. How are you holding up?"

"I'm okay. Still furious he wouldn't allow me to go with him."

"Aww… don't be. Hey, if the shoe was on the other foot, you'd be telling him the same. Go on, admit it."

Sara rolled her eyes and sighed. "You're right. Take a seat. How are things going with the wedding? Two weeks aren't long enough to get everything planned."

"I know. Remind me whose idea it was to get married on the hop?"

Sara smirked. "Since when do you usually listen to my suggestions?"

"It seemed a good idea at the time. Quiet around here lately."

"Don't say that too loud or DCI Price will hear you and start making cuts."

Carla sat in the chair opposite. "Do you think that's a possibility?"

Sara glanced out of the window at the grey skies threatening to spoil their day. "Who knows? It doesn't take much to get the ball rolling on making cuts, not these days. Is all the paperwork up to scratch? We have that farmer case coming up in a couple of weeks, so we should get that one sewn up by Friday, just in case another serial killer rears their head and decides to make our lives hell. Have I tempted fate with those words?"

Carla laughed. "More than likely. I'll make a start on the file. It should all be there, but there might be a few aspects that need clearing up, I suspect, more to do with the environmental health officer than the farmer."

"Yeah, greedy bastard. I'm glad he'll be getting his comeuppance. Despicable shithead, putting his sick wife through all that."

"And to think, she was his excuse for him getting involved. He was only trying to make her life better by accepting the bribes. What an absolute dickhead."

"Yep, he's laughing on the other side of his face now. It's the wife I feel sorry for, having to go into a home now as no one else in his family is willing to step forward and look after her."

"Everyone has their own lives to lead. I suppose they're

considering what a burden she would be to them. You can't blame them."

"I know, hard to blame them when he's the one who vowed to care for his wife through sickness and in health when they got married."

"Such a moral dilemma for all the family. Their hatred for him must overshadow their decision to care for his wife."

"Which is why no one has stepped forward to volunteer to do it. Anyway, we could sit here and debate this topic for hours and I fear still not make any headway."

"True enough. I'll leave you to it and start on the file. Anything else you need before I go?"

Sara left her seat and walked towards Carla. "A hug wouldn't go amiss right now."

Carla smiled, stood and walked into her arms. "Your wish is my command. I'm always here for you, you know that."

"I know. Thanks, Carla. And don't forget to give me a shout if you need a hand making any last-minute arrangements for your wedding."

"Ah, there is one thing."

Sara pushed away from her. "Name it."

"I'm kidding, it's all in hand, or it was, the last time I checked."

"Well, give me a shout if things become too stressed and I can do anything for you."

"Don't worry, I will." Carla smiled and left the room.

Sara paused to look at the view, not that there was much to see on a day like today with the low clouds shielding the Brecon Beacons from her, and then she sat behind her desk again. She spent the next ten minutes ploughing through her emails. She was so caught up in the task that she forgot to drink her coffee while it was still warm. The phone rang, suppressing any thoughts she had of replacing it with a fresh cup.

"DI Sara Ramsey, how may I help?"

"Sorry to disturb you, ma'am, it's Jeff, on reception."

"You haven't, not really. What can I do for you, Jeff?"

"I was wondering if you wouldn't mind having a word with a lady who has just reported her husband missing."

Sara and her team didn't usually get involved in missing person cases, not unless they were related to a murder inquiry, but she knew that Jeff only contacted her if he felt there was something more to the case than met the eye. "Okay, murder cases are a little thin on the ground at present. I'll pop down and have a word with her. Is she up for a chat with me?"

He lowered his voice and said, "She's a little distraught."

"Understandable. Give me two minutes."

"Much appreciated, thanks, ma'am. That's another one I owe you."

"Hey, they're mounting up."

He laughed and ended the call.

Sara sorted what was left of the post and shoved anything that needed a response back into the in-tray to go over later. She collected her jacket from the back of the chair and left the room. "Carla, we've got someone to meet downstairs. A missing person case."

Her partner opened her mouth, ready to object, but Sara raised a hand to cut her off.

"I trust Jeff. If he thinks it's worth us taking a gander at, then that's what I intend to do."

Carla stood. "Who am I to argue with that logic?" She picked up her notebook and pen and followed Sara out of the room and caught up with her on the stairs. "Do we know anything else?"

"Nope, that's it."

They reached the reception area to find a slim, blonde

woman waiting for them. Sara glanced over at the counter, and Jeff nodded.

"This is Mrs Pittman."

Sara smiled when the woman glanced up at her. "Mrs Pittman, or do you have a Christian name I can use?"

"It's Didi. Are you going to help me?"

"We're going to try. Is the interview room free, Sergeant?"

"It is, ma'am. Can I get anyone a drink?"

"Two coffees for us, white with one. Didi?"

"Black, no sugar for me. Thanks, that's very kind of you."

Sara showed the woman into the room off to the right, and they all sat around the small square table. Jeff brought the drinks in a little while later, and then the interview began. Didi placed her hands around her cup and stared at the contents.

"In your own time, can you tell us what happened?"

"Erik went to work as usual last Friday but didn't come home. I didn't realise until later that evening that anything was wrong because I went straight from work to my parents' house for the weekend. My father has been ill lately, and I said I'd go over there to lend a hand, you know, to give my mum a break."

Carla jotted down the notes.

"Where do your parents live?"

"In Coventry."

"Is there a reason you went alone?"

Didi stared at the contents of her mug. "Because Erik doesn't really get on with my father. They're too much alike, and it's horrendous when they're in the same room together."

"And when did you realise there was something wrong at home?"

"Not until Saturday morning. I tried to call Erik on the Friday. I couldn't get an answer, so I presumed he'd made use of his time alone and gone out with the lads. It's not the first time he's done that. Any excuse for some men, right?"

Sara smiled. "I believe so. Saturday morning came and you tried again, is that right?"

"Correct. Except I didn't receive an answer from him again. I tried him several times during the day and still no joy. I assumed he was out for the count at home, so I left it until Sunday, and when his phone kept ringing out, that's when I began to get worried. It's so unlike him not to answer his phone, even when we've fallen out with each other."

"Does that happen frequently?"

She glanced up, her gaze fixed on Sara, and nodded. "We're married, of course it does. It's par for the course, isn't it?"

Sara raised an eyebrow. *No, not every marriage is toxic.* "May I ask how long you've been married?"

"Coming up to three years. We eloped to Gretna Green. He refused to burden our parents with debt. Mum and Dad were disappointed, they had set aside some money for the wedding, so they gave us the money to put down as a deposit on our first home, instead."

"That gave you a good start to married life. When you fall out, how long does it take for you to make up and forgive each other?"

"What type of question is that? How do I know? There's no set time limit on things of that nature, is there? I suppose it depends on whether there is any kind of remorse forthcoming or if he apologises."

"It's usually down to your husband to apologise?"

"Oh, yes, because he's always in the wrong, just like most men."

Sara smiled. "And you're never to blame when you fall out, is that what you're telling us?"

"Occasionally, if I am, I always admit it. That's where we're different, he rarely admits it when he's wrong."

"And how often do you fall out with each other?"

"Once or twice a week, sometimes less and sometimes more, it depends really." Didi's head lowered, and she mumbled, "Mum always says it serves us right for eloping when we did."

"What did she mean by that?"

"Because I hadn't known him long. You know how much men like to impress you the first few months of a relationship, and then it's all downhill after that when their masks slip. That's what it has been like for us. A challenge every day, but it doesn't mean that I don't love him. I do, in my own way."

"I'm sure you do. So, when was the last time you spoke with Erik or saw him?"

"It was on Friday morning, when I was packing my overnight bag. He saw me doing that and flipped. I didn't give a shit about it at the time. It's my life, I do what I want, when I want." She held up her left hand. "Just because I have a ring on my finger, it doesn't mean I have to give up my right to have a life of my own. If my parents need me, as was the case this weekend, then I'm sorry, he's got to realise that I'm going to drop everything and go to be there with them. I'm right, aren't I? Isn't that what women do for their loved ones? It's a gender thing, isn't it? Men just don't get it, do they?"

"I'm not really sure, so can't comment on each individual relationship. My husband's mother has been ill lately, and he dropped everything to go to be with her, even closed down his business. So, every situation or relationship is different, I don't think there's a one size fits all, not really."

"Oh well. Anyway, I last saw him first thing Friday morning. He stormed off to work in a huff. He cooled down a few hours later and rang me to apologise. I gave him the cold shoulder and was really short with him. I hate it when he treats me like bloody shit, which is nine-tenths of the time."

"If that's the case, why do you stay together?"

Didi intertwined her fingers around the mug and sighed. "I suppose it's too much hassle to separate, now that we have a house in both our names and other possessions that would need to be divided up. The truth is, I love him."

Sara felt the last part of her sentence was thrown in for good measure, as an afterthought even. "I see. And when you're apart, does he usually answer his phone?"

"Yes, all the time, that's why I'm so worried about him."

"Obvious question, have you contacted all his friends and work colleagues?"

Didi lowered her head and shook it. "I can't, I don't have their numbers. Although I did ring his office today, and they told me he hadn't shown up for work. As soon as I heard that, I knew I had to come here and report him missing. I didn't know what else to do. Can you help me?"

"We're going to do our best for you. We're going to need a few details from you first, before we can begin searching for him."

"Of course. What do you need to know?"

"Is it possible that Erik might have left the family home willingly?"

"Willingly? I don't understand your question."

"Sorry, I'll rephrase the question. Do you know if he packed a bag or not?"

Didi stared at the wall ahead of her. "I'm not sure. I didn't even check. I can do that when I get back home and give you a call, if it will help?"

"Perfect. Do you have any form of security cameras at home? A video doorbell for instance?"

"No, I can't stand things like that, I see them as an intrusion to your privacy, not as a security measure. I've seen some horrendous clips on TikTok, as well as some funny ones involving doorbell video cameras, but they're not for me. Erik has been begging me to fit one recently, but I've put my foot down." She lowered her voice and added, "Maybe I'll regret that decision."

"Perhaps. We don't really know what's happened to your husband, so we won't know the answer to that. And you say you haven't got access to your husband's friends' details?"

"No, they're all in his phone. You know what it's like, all this technology is all fine and dandy if it's working properly. I guess we never stop to think what turmoil our lives would be in if we ever mislay or lose our phones. Lesson learnt for me, I'm going to go through my contact list and start jotting down everyone's details in either a notebook or address book."

"It's always best to have a backup of any important information you might need in the future. Do you remember any of his friends' names or where they might live?"

"No, not really. He had nicknames for all of them. I couldn't possibly tell you their real names."

"Have you ever met any of them?"

"Once or twice, again, he introduced me to his mates by their nicknames, and I'm afraid I haven't got the patience for such nonsense, so it went in one ear and straight out the other. I know that's no help to you and I'm sorry about that."

"Don't be, as detectives these things are always sent to try us. We'll overcome this obstacle, at least, I hope we will. Can you tell us where he works?"

Didi removed a slip of paper from her pocket and slid it across the table. "I was prepared for you asking that. I can never remember the name of the firm, so I wrote it down just in case you needed it."

Sara read the details out loud. "Thirlwell Consultants.

And what does his job entail?" She had an idea that Didi wouldn't be able to tell her.

"Umm... he's an IT consultant, that's as much as I can tell you, I'm sorry."

Sara gave her a reassuring smile. "It's fine, don't worry. We'll pay them a visit after we've finished here, see what they can tell us. Has your husband fallen out with anyone lately? A work colleague, one of his friends, or even a neighbour perhaps?"

Didi shook her head. "If he had he didn't tell me. He wasn't really one for general chitchat."

In other words, you barely knew your husband, his likes and dislikes, and the people he hung around with. Or anything else for that matter. "Is there anything else you can tell us?"

"No, that's everything, I think. There's bound to be something I've missed. Maybe I can call you later if anything else comes to mind?"

"I'll give you one of my cards." Sara gave her one and then asked, "What about your husband's car?"

Didi frowned and took a sip of her now-cooled drink. "What about it?"

"What type of car does he drive? Have you seen it since he went missing?"

"Gosh, okay, now you're testing me. There's a car park opposite the firm. I didn't think to go and check to see if it's still there. That makes me sound awful, doesn't it?"

"Not at all. You've been worried, that tends to cloud people's judgement if they're concerned about their loved one. Any idea of the make and model?"

"I don't know. I have a Mini and I'm not really bothered about what hubby drives. It's a big one, a four-wheel jobbie, I think. I know, I'm hopeless. I'm as much use as a chocolate teapot and I'm probably making your job a lot harder than it needs to be. I was reluctant about coming here today because

I thought I wouldn't be able to give you the answers that you need."

"Stop apologising, it's fine. If you give us your husband's full name and address, we can check the system and get the answers we need from that."

"Thank God. I run a successful online clothing business, and my head is so full of that shit most of the time that everything else seems to be pushed aside. I feel bad about it, but the business is very lucrative and deserves a lot of my attention. It's at times like this, though, that I realise what I'm missing out on in life. I've always been a workaholic, but where does it really get us in the end?"

"Don't beat yourself up about this. You've done the right thing coming in today and reporting your husband missing. What's his full name and address?"

"It's Erik, with a K, Pittman. We live at five Dove Way out at Creddenhill. It's a relatively new estate of executive houses."

"I think I know the ones. Have you lived there long?"

"Since they were built, so two years. It's really peaceful around there. I hated the thought of living on a large estate, so we paid extra for this house. They were built by a builder with a solid reputation, not one of these large concerns who take your money and run at the first sign of trouble. I was put off buying a new-build for years when I saw an undercover programme about one of the big firms, can't remember their name now. I agreed to go ahead with our house but only if we had input along the way. The builder welcomed our point of view, and we adapted the property to our needs for the same cost. I couldn't see one of the big housebuilding companies doing that. My friend bought a Dale Windsor home, and two months after she moved in the stairs collapsed. They turned out to be made out of MDF, can you believe that? Disgusting, it was, and they kicked up a right fuss about replacing it, too, only agreed to carry out repairs on it."

"That's terrible. Yes, I've heard some building companies are getting bad reputations. I have a new-build, well, it's a few years old now, but again, like you, the small estate was built by a local builder who cares about his reputation and his customers. Okay, is there anything else you can tell us that you think we should know?"

Carla scribbled something in her notebook and slid it towards Sara.

She read it and nodded. "Sorry, my partner has just reminded me that we know nothing about his family. Does he have any siblings? Or other family members living nearby?"

"No, he's not from round here, he's from Manchester. He only moved here about six years ago. He doesn't have any brothers or sisters, and his mum cut him off because he refused to go to his father's funeral. From what I can tell, his father used to chase him around the house with a belt, beat him black and blue if he ever said anything he shouldn't have."

"Nice man. I think I would have refused to have attended his funeral as well. Okay, I think we're done here now."

"Will you keep me informed on how the case proceeds?"

"Yes, if that's what you want. Like I said, we'll pop over to his place of work now, see if we can find out anything there. I can give you a call later if anything of interest comes to light."

"Thank you. It's the not knowing that is eating away at me."

"I can imagine. Try not to fret about it, we'll do our best to bring him back to you."

"I hope so. It's true what they say, you don't realise what you've got until it's gone."

And yet you were picking fault in him earlier, acting as if you couldn't stand him. Sara nodded. "I know. Keep thinking positively, and I'm confident you'll be reunited with Erik soon."

Didi wiped a tear from her eye, and they all stood. Carla walked towards the security door while Sara showed Didi out to her car.

"Thank you again for seeing me and agreeing to take the case on. The sergeant I spoke to when I arrived told me that you're the best police officer at the station. I hope he's right."

"There's no need for you to worry, my team and I are utter professionals. We won't let you down, I promise."

"I hope that's the case. I need my husband back."

Sara held the car door open, and Didi slid behind the steering wheel. She smiled up at her and mouthed 'thank you' again. Sara waved her off and then darted back into the station just as the heavens opened.

"Damn weather. We've had nothing but rain lately. Remind me when spring is supposed to arrive?"

Jeff snorted. "According to the weathermen it's just around the corner, but they've been known to get it wrong in the past."

"Yeah, haven't they just? Thanks for giving me a shout about the case."

"I wasn't sure if you'd be interested or not. I had a hunch, glad it paid off. She seems a nice lady, very distraught, which is understandable in the circumstances."

"Hopefully, what I had to say reassured her. I'd better go upstairs and make a start."

"I've told her she'll be in safe hands with you."

"I'm glad you have faith in our abilities."

"Get away with you. It's not like you to doubt yourself, ma'am."

She held her hand out and waved it from side to side. "It's

a struggle at times, especially when I have personal baggage weighing me down."

"Damn, it slipped my mind. How is Mark?"

"He's bearing up. He's due to start his treatment today. Even more reason to throw myself into the case. I'm relishing the distraction. He assured me everything is going to be okay and refused point-blank to let me take him to the hospital this morning."

"You'll be there when he comes home, he'll be grateful for that."

"With bells on. I'll pass on your best wishes."

"You do that."

Sara unlocked the security door and trudged up the stairs, Mark's treatment and what lay ahead of him uppermost in her mind, as she knew it would be throughout the next couple of weeks until he rang the bell at the hospital. Whether he wanted her there or not, she intended to show up to support him and rejoice in his excitement on that euphoric day. Sadness had touched their lives all too often over the past couple of years, what with her having to say farewell to her mum, and Mark's mother also ending up in hospital with a brain tumour. She'd had surgery and was still with them, but it had left her with limited mobility. Her speech had been significantly affected, but the oncologist was hopeful that with therapy she would make a full recovery. It was the boost they'd needed as a family and gave Mark the courage to share his devastating news with his father. Between them, they had decided to keep his prognosis from his mother until she turned a corner in her own health.

She entered the incident room as Carla punched the air. "Yes, I've got it."

Sara cocked her head. "His car?"

Grinning, her partner said, "Well, the make, model and reg, that's something, isn't it?"

"That's one step closer. Forgive me if I don't jump for joy just yet, though. What is it?"

"A Subaru Outback."

"Come on then, what are we waiting for?"

Carla shot out of her chair and pulled on her jacket, and they left the station.

THIRLWELL CONSULTANTS WAS a distinctive building in the centre of the city, near to the courtroom and all the solicitors' offices.

"That must be the car park Didi mentioned. We'll check in there first, before we go in and have a word with his colleagues."

They parked in a space close to the front and searched the area. They found Erik's Subaru in a spot at the rear.

Sara tried to open the driver's door, but it was locked. "Worth a try. I wonder if we can get a good view in the back."

"There's one way of finding out."

They shifted to the rear of the vehicle. Again, the door was locked, and there was no sign of life inside. Sara scanned the area and spotted a CCTV camera at the entrance and one at the rear.

"There's only one way in and out, which is unusual. Let's see if the footage can tell us more."

With the rain now lashing down, they hurried across the road and shook off the excess in the foyer of the office building. A receptionist glanced their way but didn't offer to help them until they approached the large desk that was made of glass and chrome.

"Can I help you, ladies?"

Sara and Carla flashed their IDs, and Sara introduced them.

"We're here to see the person in charge of Thirlwell Consultants."

"Oh, I see. I'll have to make a call, check if Mr Boyce is available before I allow you upstairs. He's an extremely busy man."

Sara smiled at the receptionist. "Aren't we all…? Busy, I mean."

"Oh, yes, of course you are," the receptionist stuttered. "I didn't mean to presume otherwise. I won't be a moment. Why don't you take a seat over there?"

Sara and Carla gave the receptionist the room she needed to make the call but didn't sit on the padded chairs for fear of getting them wet.

"I feel like the proverbial drowned rat," Sara complained.

"I have news for you, you look like one."

"So do you. There's a mirror over there, you might want to check it out."

Carla pulled a face at her.

The receptionist clicked her fingers to gain their attention. They deliberately ignored the rude gesture.

In the end, the receptionist called out to them, "Officers, can you come back to the desk?"

Sara smiled as she walked towards the pretty woman with sleek black hair draping over each shoulder. "Hello again. Any news for us?"

"Yes, Mr Boyce said he has a slot to see you now, but it will only be for five minutes. If that isn't suitable for your needs, he has another slot free at three this afternoon, if you'd prefer."

"Now is fine. We shouldn't keep him too long."

"Okay, I'll ask the security guard to show you the way. Terry, can you take the officers upstairs to Mr Boyce's office for me, please?"

The burly older man left his position behind the small

desk close to the revolving door and smiled as he came towards them. "I sure can. If you'd like to come with me, ladies."

"Thanks."

Once he'd summoned the lift, the guard stood back and allowed Sara and Carla to enter before him. Then he jumped on board and hit the button for the top floor. "It shouldn't take us too long. Thankfully, the lift is ultra reliable."

"Gosh, I'd rather you didn't tempt fate. The idea of getting stuck in one of these terrifies me," Sara said, totally serious to the extent that she'd had several nightmares to that effect over the years. In her teens, she'd spent a day at a charity event in the town, carrying out the role of escorting people to the lift and riding it up and down for a number of hours. She couldn't remember exactly how long, but it was at least two hours. Her stomach had lurched every time the lift started moving and came to a standstill again.

The trip up brought back so many uncomfortable memories for her that when they left the enclosed space, Carla tugged on her arm and asked, "Are you all right? You've gone a bit green. You're not going to throw up, are you?"

"I'm fine now I'm out of there. I'll fill you in later. We'll be taking the stairs down, if that's all right?"

"Sure. I never knew you had an aversion to riding a lift, is that something new? I can't say I've noticed it before."

"It hits me periodically; this happens to be one of those days."

The security guard accompanied them to the main office on that floor and left them after he'd introduced them to Boyce who was waiting in his outer office with his secretary.

The man was in his mid-fifties. Smartly dressed in a grey pin-striped suit. He shook their hands and showed them into his office where he sat in his executive chair behind his glass desk. Sara suspected the view out of the floor-to-ceiling window would have been exceptional if it hadn't been for the rain battering it.

"Nice weather we're having. It would appear that spring has been delayed for yet another year. Always the same, eh? The winters are getting longer and the summers shorter. I suppose we can blame climate change for that. Anyway, that's a topic that could last for hours, and as I only have five minutes to spare, even less now, we'd better leave it. What can I do for you?"

"First of all, I'd like to thank you for agreeing to see us today. The reason we're here is because we're concerned about a member of your staff, Erik Pittman."

He frowned. "Has he done something wrong? I've never had a problem with his work ethic or anything else in the past."

"His wife has just reported him as a missing person. Apparently, she hasn't seen him since Friday morning."

"Oh, I wasn't aware he was missing. Hold on, let me give his line manager a call." He picked up the phone. "Alan, can you pop up and see me for a moment? Yes, it's an urgent matter. Okay, I'll see you soon." He held up a finger. "Let me get my secretary to rearrange my schedule for the next thirty minutes."

"Thank you, I'd appreciate that."

True to his word, Boyce postponed his next two appointments, and Alan joined them a few minutes later.

"Come in, Alan. These two officers have been instructed to look into a missing person case."

"Oh, sounds intriguing, how can I help?"

"The person concerned is Erik Pittman. Can you tell us when you last saw him?"

"Bugger, he's not at work today. I was going to leave it until eleven before I chased him up. It's unlike him not to show up for work. He was here on Friday, worked all day as far as I can remember. In fact, I believe he was still working when I clocked off at six. I had a dinner arrangement I couldn't get out of on Friday evening. I'm usually the one to leave last."

"The thing is, his vehicle is still parked across the road," Sara said. "Do you know if he had any plans for Friday night? We know his wife was away for the weekend at her parents'."

Alan shook his head. "If he did, he didn't tell me. I could see if any of the other staff were aware of his plans."

"That would be great, thanks."

"Use the phone, Alan," Boyce said.

He did, but the result remained the same. Erik hadn't told anyone what his plans were for Friday evening.

"That's a shame," Sara said. "Not to worry. I noticed there are a couple of cameras overlooking the car park. Do you have access to the footage?"

"Yes, it's our car park. I can arrange for you to view it with the security guard if that would help?" Mr Boyce said obligingly.

"It would, we can do that afterwards. I'd like to know if Erik ever mentioned if he was having any problems, either with a colleague or at home."

Alan shuffled in his seat. "I hope I'm not speaking out of turn when I tell you this, but I don't think he has the best of marriages. His wife runs her own business from home, and Erik complains constantly about how much of her time it consumes, to the extent that she never does anything around the house. And no, that's not a sexist comment, I mean she did absolutely nothing, despite being at home all day. He told me that he had to employ a cleaner a few months ago and even then, the house never seemed to be that clean because his wife refused to clear the rooms of all the stock she holds. The chaos hampered the cleaner from doing her job properly. The last I heard was that she'd jacked it in, frustrated that she wasn't allowed to carry out her chores correctly without Didi jumping down her throat."

Carla jotted down the information. "Interesting, so it caused a lot of friction between husband and wife then?"

"And some. I think he was on the verge of asking for a divorce. I know they had words last month and Didi promised to mend her ways and keep the home tidy. There was talk of her transferring all of her stock to a warehouse or a storage unit."

"And when did this happen?"

"At the beginning of last month. I think it took Didi a few weeks to come around to the idea. I know he spent a weekend shifting the gear to a new storage unit, but I also know it put a severe strain on their marriage at the same time."

Sara nodded. "But things have been all right between them ever since, have they?"

"I'm not sure, I can't say Erik ever mentioned it again. I think he was relieved to get his house back and not have all the stress of weaving his way through the gear to get to sit down in the lounge every night."

"Apart from that incident, would you say they had a happy marriage before that?"

"I suppose a bit like any other couple I know. Arguments here and there, and they spent a lot of time making up with each other. Let's just say, every time he started telling me about his home life it reinforced the reason why I enjoy being single. I lost my wife to cancer a couple of years ago."

"Sorry to hear that," Sara said. "And there's been no one else in your life since?"

"No, my wife was a very special person. We'd been together since we met at school, no one could hold a candle to her. Broke my heart when I lost her. I can't see it mending anytime soon either. I survive on my own; we learn to adapt, don't we? For the greater good, especially when I see what the alternatives are like. My wife and I never had a cross word, not in the twenty-two years we were married."

"Sorry to hear of your loss. Maybe someone will come into your life and change your perception when you least expect it. I'm living proof that can happen, after the death of my first husband. But that's by the by."

"It did? Sorry to hear of your loss."

Sara waved a hand. "Don't be. There are people out there who are able to sweep us off our feet when we least expect them to, so never give up hope."

He smiled. "I fear I'm too set in my ways now to accept someone else to share my life with. I'm happy enough. I'm fortunate that I love my job. It's great to have the freedom to work longer hours if I need to on a project or come in at the weekend if I have to go over something that is bugging me, rather than sit at home, letting it drive me crazy. It doesn't occur that often, but I'm grateful that I'm single when such dilemmas crop up."

"I can vouch for Alan, he's very committed to his career, which is a huge benefit to the company. Is there anything else you need to know?" Mr Boyce said.

"What was Erik's relationship like with his clients, or customers would you call them?"

Alan cleared his throat. "Clients. I have to say he was exceptional. Always went the extra mile for them. We've had no complaints to the contrary since he began working for us."

"And how long has that been?"

"Around ten years, give or take a few months. He's one of our top consultants. I've recently put him forward for a promotion, isn't that right, Mr Boyce?"

"That's right. I have a senior manager role coming up in the next month or so. I asked Alan here to sound Erik out about the position, but discreetly. You know what it's like touting a job that isn't vacant yet. It's not really the done thing, is it?"

"I can understand that. So, he had a lot to look forward to in his career, no reason for him to take off and leave his position at the firm?"

"None whatsoever in my eyes," Boyce replied.

"I second that," Alan said.

"Then I think we've covered everything. If we can have a word with the security guard and perhaps view the footage, then our job here is done."

Alan rose from his seat. "If you'd like to come with me."

Sara and Carla both stood.

Sara reached out a hand to Mr Boyce. "Thank you for seeing us at short notice."

"My pleasure. I hope Erik is all right and that you find him soon."

They followed Alan out of the office.

"Umm... would it be possible for us to take the stairs? I'm not keen on travelling in the lift," Sara said.

"Of course. Here we go." He pushed open the door closest to him, and they spent the next ten minutes winding their way down a steep staircase to the reception area again. "You'll be needing a cuppa after your exertions," Alan joked.

"A coffee wouldn't go amiss, if there's one going," Sara agreed.

"Let me see if Lucy can arrange that for you while I have a word with Terry." He stopped at the reception desk.

Lucy nodded and left her seat. "Two coffees? How do you take them?" the receptionist asked.

"White with one sugar in both, thanks."

Alan had a quiet word with Terry who stood as he approached.

"Sure, I can see what I can find. Don is due to take over from me soon, if the ladies are prepared to wait?"

"Are you?" Alan turned to ask.

"Fine by us. Especially if we have a drink to occupy us."

"That's settled then. I'll leave you in Terry's capable hands. Good luck." Alan smiled and mock saluted, then called for the lift to take him back to his office.

Lucy handed them a mug of coffee each, and they took a seat in the padded chairs now that they'd rid themselves of the excess rain.

"What did you make of what we learnt about the marriage?" Carla asked. She blew on her drink and took a sip.

"Hard to tell. If we hadn't already met Didi I'd be suspicious of her, but having spent half an hour in her presence and hearing how concerned she is about her husband, I can't see there being anything we should be worried about. You?"

"Yeah, I thought the same. According to his boss, there doesn't seem to be any reason why he should have gone missing. It sounds like it's going to be yet another complex case for us to solve."

"Nothing new there then." Sara laughed.

Another guard came through the revolving door, and the two men shared a joke before the new arrival drifted into a nearby room and re-emerged a few minutes later. He slapped Terry on the back and took over the post at the front door.

Terry crossed the reception area to join them. "I'm ready when you are, ladies. No rush. Come through to my office when you've finished your drinks, it's the door over on the right there."

"We won't be long, unless we can bring our coffees with us?"

"Sure, go for it."

The three of them crossed the marble entrance to the security office.

"It's not too small in here. Let me arrange the seats better."

"We've been squished into smaller offices over the years," Sara quipped.

He placed three seats in front of the four monitors and chose the one closest to the controls for himself. "Let's see what we can find for you. Can you give me an idea of what time and day you're searching for?"

"Sorry, yes, Friday, although we're not sure of the time. Do you know at what time they knock off around here?"

"Hmm... Friday can be different to the other days. You know, people intent on tying up loose ends before the weekend means they often run over. Let's see what six o'clock comes up with and we'll go from there."

Sara sipped at her drink and watched the staff leaving the building and making their way over to the car park. "Are the parking slots over the road designated for the staff only?"

"They are. The firm used to allow all and sundry to park over there, but the public took the piss and the staff ended up missing out and struggling to find spaces close by. So, Mr Boyce said enough was enough and closed it to the public."

"Makes sense as parking is at a premium in the city centre."

They fell silent and observed several staff members leave the building.

It was then that Sara realised she hadn't asked Didi for a photo of her husband. "I'm going to be relying on you to identify Erik Pittman, Terry."

"It's okay. It shouldn't be a problem."

He sped through the recording and then stopped at six-twenty. "Ah, what's this? Yep, this is Erik. He's crossing the road to collect his car."

They watched him get in his vehicle and drive to the exit, only to have a van pull up and block his way.

"Shit! This has an ominous feel about it," Terry suggested.

"Hmm... you're not wrong. There are three masked people. He didn't stand a chance."

The gang clobbered him, knocked him to the ground, and then, between them, they struggled to get his limp body into the back of the van. After a few failed attempts, they finally managed it. Then one of the gang members jumped in Erik's vehicle and reversed it to the rear of the car park. The lights flashed as the car was locked, then the person ran and dived into the back of the van before it sped off.

Sara leaned forward in her seat. "Bugger, so that's how he ended up on the missing list. He was bloody knocked out cold and abducted. Can we focus on the van, get the make, colour and reg, if it's available?"

"Leave it with me, I'm a dab hand at tweaking images." He fiddled with the controls. The image was enlarged, but the angle of the cameras failed to capture the registration number.

"Does it even have one?" Carla asked. She left her chair and got closer to the screen. "I can't see one."

Terry tutted and sucked in a sharp breath. "I was about to say the same, I thought my eyes were deceiving me."

"Not helpful. This reeks of being premeditated." Sara groaned.

"You mean he was intentionally targeted?" Terry asked.

Sara nodded. "Seems that way. All we need to find out now is why. Have you seen the van before? Perhaps seen it hanging around the car park, maybe out there doing a trial run over the past few weeks?"

Terry sighed. "I don't recognise it. As for seeing it before, now you're asking. I can't say I've noticed it, but then, I wasn't really looking out for it, was I? Sorry, that's no help, is it?"

"Not to worry. Can we get a copy of the recording?"

"Give me two minutes."

Sara and Carla left the room and paced the reception area outside until Terry handed Sara the disc.

"Thanks, Terry. You've been a huge help in our investigation."

"It's part and parcel of the job. I hope it helps you get Mr Pittman back. He's a decent bloke, from what I know of him. I wouldn't have earmarked him as any kind of troublemaker."

"Let's hope we find him soon."

Sara drove back to the station and set the footage up for all the team to view on the fifty-inch screen they had at their disposal.

"I hate to say this," Craig said hesitantly.

"Go on, don't be afraid to voice your opinion."

"I'm getting the impression we're looking at three women. Their builds for a start, and the lack of strength they seem to have, tossing him in the back of the van. It's not as if he's carrying any excess weight, is it?"

Sara rubbed at her chin and replayed the footage another couple of times; each time, his theory grew increasingly viable. "I think you're right. Anyone else think the same?"

"The more you play it, the more convinced I'm becoming," Carla added. "What the fuck? Well, this is new for us, apart from that one case I seem to recall."

"Where the women made a murder pact to kill off each other's husband?" Sara said after a moment's hesitation.

Carla tapped the side of the nose. "Which brings us back to Didi, or does it?"

"Hmm... let's not jump the gun on that one just yet. We're going to need substantial evidence before we can go round there and accuse her of the unthinkable."

"The person who parked the car seemed to know how to drive it well," Carla suggested.

"That's still not enough for us to drop any charges on her. Okay, you know what I'm going to ask you to do next, Craig, don't you?"

"You want me to follow the van's progress through the city via the ANPR cameras and get back to you ASAP."

Sara smiled and winked at him. Then viewed the footage again, noting if any of the assailants spoke to Erik or not. It was hard to tell with the three people wearing balaclavas. "They came prepared and targeted him for a reason, that much is evident. All we need to do now is find out why? The firm couldn't shed any light on any of this, and we're up shit creek regarding any friends he might have as the wife told us that she knows these people just by their nicknames. Not helpful in the slightest. So, we're going to be reliant on you, Craig, to come up with the goods."

"No pressure there, boss. I'll do my best."

"Will, be prepared to give him a hand if required. I have a feeling we're going to need to find Erik swiftly, if it's not too late already."

CHAPTER 4

Chelsey paced the floor until the other girls arrived at the house. It was five-fifteen. She had already been upstairs to check on the captive. He was dozing and hadn't stirred when she had quietly entered the room. She collected the empty bowl from the cereals she'd dropped by and given him on the way to work that morning. She'd also supplied him with a sandwich wrapped in clingfilm; half of it remained uneaten.

Polly was the next to arrive. She was still dressed in her baker's uniform. "I got here as quickly as I could. I'm not going to apologise for being late, duty called and all that. We had a late delivery of flour that I had to attend to as the boss failed to show up this afternoon. No damn call to tell me she was going to be late, miserable effing cow. She's always taking the piss, expecting me to deal with that kind of shit all the time."

"Not good, hon. Sorry she treats you so badly. Hang on to that anger, we might need it in a while."

Polly frowned and inclined her head. "Why? What are your intentions?"

Chelsey's gaze drifted up to the ceiling, and Polly shook her head.

"You're not going to hurt him, are you?"

Chelsey folded her arms and tapped her foot. "Name me one good reason why we shouldn't! We've had him here all weekend, and he's barely said a bloody word to us. It's time we upped the ante."

"Do we have to? You know how I feel about violence. I can't even watch a movie if there's any sign of aggression or blood in it."

"Don't be such a wimp. Needs must in this case. He knows something, I can see it in his eyes. It's time for him to tell us, give up a name, or suffer the consequences."

The front door slammed, and Tammy entered the room in her sports gear. "I'll have to make this quick, I'm doing a double shift today. I told the boss I had to nip home to see to my cat."

"But you haven't got a cat," Polly said naively.

Tammy and Chelsey both suppressed a snigger.

"Exactly, I've had to invent one so I could get time off to be here, numpty," Tammy said.

Polly's cheeks coloured up. "Oh. All right, I'm slow on the uptake, there's no need for you to be nasty. I get enough of that at work, without you both jumping on the bandwagon. Give me a frigging break for a change."

"Sorry, it's been a long day, and I have another four hours ahead of me. Can we get on with this?" Tammy hugged Polly and then gave her a friendly punch to the arm.

"I think we should. We've been more than patient with the bastard, and he's still not provided us with the information we need, so it's time to notch things up a bit," Chelsey said.

Polly swallowed. "I didn't sign up for this. Can't we do it without using force or violence?"

"Are you for real?" Chelsey said. "You read our notes, you knew what to expect. Don't go soft on us now, Polly."

"I'm not," Polly bristled. "You know I can't abide any form of violence, especially if he's innocent. Don't you think he would have revealed the truth by now if he knew it?"

"Men have a special bond. They stick together like Super Glue. It's going to be down to us to prise them apart," Tammy replied. She made a shredding motion with her hands to emphasize her point.

"I'm beginning to wish I had gone straight home tonight, I just know it," Polly grumbled.

"The sooner we get on with things the better," Chelsey said. Metal bar in hand, she led the way up the stairs to the bedroom where Erik was being held.

They entered the room noisily on purpose, and he shot up in bed. His hands and feet were tied; they hadn't bothered placing anything over his mouth because the house was detached and in the middle of nowhere. Ideal for their purpose.

"Right, this is your final chance to tell us what you know, Erik. We've been patient with you up until now, and that's run out," Chelsey said. She moved closer to the bed and struck the metal bar into the palm of her left hand.

He squirmed and hunkered up against the wall. "I don't know anything. You can't do this to me."

"Can't we? I can tell a liar from fifty paces, mate. This is your last chance to confess all or my friend, Mr Bar here, is going to make a mess of your legs, and he won't hold back, I can assure you."

Tammy stepped forward to stand alongside Chelsey and leaned in. "Tell us and we'll let you go, it's as simple as that."

"I don't fucking know. Why won't you sodding believe me? You think I want to get my legs broken? I don't, I would tell you to avoid you bashing me."

His whining voice made Chelsey's toes curl. To her ear, it was false and unconvincing. "Right, girls. Hold his legs still."

Tammy was the first to reach for Erik's legs. He kicked out and wriggled as much as he was able to, but the rope tied around his ankles hindered his ability to move.

"Polly, either get involved or get out of the room," Tammy shouted as she struggled to get hold of Erik's moving limbs.

"I can't," Polly said and bolted for the door.

"Fucking shit!" Tammy shouted.

"We can do it between us. I'll help you straighten his legs and then you can sit on his ankles while I beat seven bells of shit out of him," Chelsey said. The adrenaline pumped through her veins, as if egging her on.

"No, no, don't do this. There must be something I can say or do that will change your minds," Erik pleaded, his voice frantically rising several octaves as the fear took over.

"Yeah, there is. You know what we're after, the truth. Tell me who raped me, and all this could be avoided."

"It wasn't me. I swear. So you have no need to do this to me. I'm not a rapist, I never have been."

"But we know what guys are like, they share secrets, laugh behind women's backs. I can hear you all now, laughing behind *my* back. Well, I have news for you, you're not going to get away with this, none of you are. We're going to round you all up until one of you tells us the truth. Until one of you has the decency to step forward and admit to what he's done."

"I'm not the guilty party. You have no right taking this out on me."

"I'm tired of going over old ground. You've had all weekend to reveal the truth. Instead, here you are, pleading with us to let you go. It's simple, give us a name and we'll set you free."

Erik's eyes widened. The whites were bloodshot through

lack of sleep. "I don't know, and that's the truth. You can't get blood out of a stone. No one has been laughing about you behind your backs. I'm sorry someone raped you, if that's what happened. You guys, all of you, were pretty drunk that night."

"My drink was spiked, and you're aware of that. There's no way I would have stripped down to my underwear in a strange house, ever. What do you take me for? Someone messed with my drink with the intention of getting their end away that night, and I was the damn target. I still feel physically sick just thinking about it. Give me a fucking name or say goodbye to the use of your legs, because I'm warning you now, once I get started, there will be no stopping me."

His face reddened, and his eyes grew wider still. "I swear I'm telling you the truth. You'll regret doing this, and that's a promise."

Chelsey nodded at Tammy. Together, they pounced on Erik and managed to overpower him. His legs were pulled straight, and Tammy sat across his calves. She swayed slightly as he squirmed like a fat worm beneath her, but it didn't prove to be much of a deterrent. Chelsey raised the bar above her head and swung at his thighs, not once, twice, or even three times. She clobbered him over and over, oblivious to his cries for help and his screams as the pain consumed his lower limbs.

"No, stop. I had nothing to do with this."

His words, or lies, incensed her even more. Annoyed that he was still refusing to divulge the truth, she pounded the bar against his thighs another couple of times.

Tammy laughed and watched the onslaught. "Do it. Punish him."

Chelsey paused. "Shit, I forgot to do the test on him."

"Fuck. Where is it?"

"In my pocket." Chelsey withdrew the HIV test and

recapped the instructions she had read through several times before coming to the house. The test had been purchased at her local chemist. She'd actually bought five of them from different assistants over the past couple of days. "Hold him still while I take a swab."

She rammed the long cotton bud into his mouth as he opened it to object and ran it around his gums, top and bottom.

"There, that should do. The results will come through in twenty minutes or so. We're done with him… for now. We can give him another bashing tomorrow and the day after until we break him."

"No, please. I need to get to the hospital; you can't leave me like this. I can tell my bones are broken; they're going to need immediate attention."

"Go fuck yourself. You'll be lucky if you get out of here alive, Erik. Think about that when you're lying here in the dark overnight, writhing in agony, too scared to move."

"I'm fucking innocent, how many more times do I have to tell you that?"

"You might be innocent, the test will give us the answer, but I still maintain you know who raped me. You know we mean business, we've already proved that, now it's your turn to spill the beans and reveal the truth."

"I can't because I don't bloody know it. Don't you think I would have told you by now?"

Chelsey shrugged and then helped Tammy to wriggle off his legs. He screamed, and they both stared at him.

"We're well aware of how much you guys cover each other's back. Think about this while we're away. Your punishment is only going to get ten times worse if you keep schtum." Chelsey picked up the test from the floor and walked towards the door.

"What's that for?" he shouted after her.

"Ah, wouldn't you like to know? Actually, I'll tell you this, it's a form of truth test."

"There's no such thing," he replied.

"Isn't there? Believe me, there is. We'll find out soon enough, don't fret about that." Chelsey allowed Tammy to pass her then slammed the door and locked it. She smiled at her friend. "I don't think he knows anything, but it was fun making him squirm like that."

"You're an evil bitch, and I love you for it. It's Polly we have to be wary about."

"I know. We're going to need to keep a watchful eye on her from now on."

"I thought she'd got over her concerns and seemed pretty chilled at the weekend while we've been here."

"It's the violence she can't hack. It's all right for her, she wasn't raped. It screws with your head. You know I haven't had a violent bone in my body, not until today. It eats away at you. It's so hard to describe. If I'd just been raped, and I don't mean that to sound flippant, not in the slightest, I think I would have been able to cope with it, but it's the HIV that repulses me. Some fucker has screwed up my life for good, and they have to pay for it. Whether that goes against the grain with Polly or not, it's something I need to punish the son of a bitch for. He had no right infecting me, and don't tell me he didn't know what he was doing, I refuse to believe it."

"Hey, I'm on your side, Chels. I can't imagine what this has done to your thinking or mental state but I'm going to stand right beside you every step of the way."

"Even when we get to your fella?"

Tammy chewed on her lower lip. "That remains to be seen. We might know the truth before then. I can't see Oscar being the guilty party. As far as I know, he didn't leave the bedroom all night."

Chelsey raised her eyebrows. "How do you know?

Weren't you out for the count for most of the night? What if your final drink was spiked like mine? Who's to say what the men got up to when we were all out cold? Maybe you should get tested yourself."

"Fucking hell, don't say that."

"Why not? You might have it as well. Take a test home with you and check. I can always get another one from the chemist to replace it. I'm willing to shoulder the cost, if that's what it takes."

"Bugger. What about Polly? Do you think she should take a test as well?"

"No harm in it. At least we'll be able to rule it out, if they prove negative."

Tammy covered her face with her hands. "Oh God, oh God, I don't think I want to know. Look how it has affected your life."

"The choice is yours. Don't get stressed about it. I know if I were in your position, I'd want to know what's going on with my body."

"All right. I'll take one home with me tonight."

They wandered back downstairs and searched for Polly. They found her in the kitchen, staring out of the patio doors at the garden.

"I couldn't bear the screams, so I found the furthest point in the house. It didn't work, so I ended up in the garden. I've just come in because it started raining. I can't cope with this, girls. Don't force me to get involved in the torture side of things. I don't mind abducting them, but I refuse to hurt them, like you do. I haven't got it in me to do it. There's no need for it."

"What? If he's lying up there, refusing to tell us the truth, then there's every bloody need to clout him. I can guarantee he knows who raped me. Anyone want a drink?" Chelsey poured herself a vodka and orange.

"No thanks. This isn't the time to be celebrating," Polly admonished her.

"I'm not. It's thirsty work bashing seven bells out of someone."

Polly slapped her hands over her ears. "La, la, la, I don't want to know the ins and outs of what you got up to in the bedroom."

Chelsey ignored Polly's childish behaviour and turned her attention to the test. She read the instructions again and noticed that there was a prominent line showing next to the C which meant the test had been successful, but there was nothing showing next to the T yet, not even a faint line. She checked her watch. "I think it's too early to get a result yet."

"I can't hang around. I need to get back to work. Are we still on for tomorrow night?" Tammy said.

"Yes, we've got the details of the second victim and where he works, we'll be waiting outside his office."

"Oh no, does it have to be so soon?" Polly asked.

"Yes, we're going to pick them all up. Have them here, together, by the end of this week. That was the plan, and we intend to stick to it," Chelsey snapped, her patience wearing thinner every time Polly complained.

"Well, pardon me for breathing. I only asked."

"I'm going to leave you to it," Tammy said. She blew them both a kiss and ran into the hallway.

"I'll give you a call later. No, you ring me when you get home, and we'll run through the details for tomorrow. Thanks for your help tonight, Tammy."

"Believe me, the pleasure was all mine. I'll do the test later as well, make sure Polly does one, too."

"What's that? What test? No way am I taking one of those. Why? Why should I? I wouldn't be able to put myself through the torture. Don't ask me to do that, please, Chels."

"It's entirely up to you. I think you would be foolish to

rule it out. Tammy is in agreement with me. Can you truthfully remember everything that happened that night? She can't, not fully, and I know my drink was spiked. You really believe I would have let a man near me that night if I was fully conscious? It was all planned, the attack on me, the spiking of the drinks. All of it. I wouldn't have put it past the group to make sure you two hitched up with a couple of fellas, ensuring you were otherwise engaged, while one of the evil bastards dropped his trousers and carried out the vile deed on me."

"That's a warped suggestion."

"Is it? No more warped than spiking someone's drink, raping them and infecting them with a life-threatening disease, or are you forgetting about the HIV aspect to this crime? Because that's what it is, it's a crime to knowingly *infect someone, me,* with what could be a fatal disease, without giving me the option to refuse sexual intercourse."

Polly sank into a nearby chair and placed her head in her hands. "Stop it, I can't listen to this any more."

"What? You're trying to block out the truth? Why? Because it's not happening to you, is that it?"

Polly dropped her hands and glared at her. "Don't be so ridiculous. We're in this together, we agreed to help you all we could."

"So why didn't you then? Up there, before when we tortured Erik? All for one, that's our motto, and yet you ran out of the room, unable to accept what was about to take place. You're a coward, through and through, Polly. Do the test, and I hope for your sake it comes back negative, because honestly, I doubt if you would cope if it came back positive. Answer me this, did you wear a condom that night?"

"Yes, of course we did and every time since."

Her eyes darted off to the left, and Chelsey sensed that Polly was lying to her. But she decided to leave it there, tired from her exertions and constant battle of wills with someone she considered to be her best friend. "Whatever. I have to go home now; I think a soak in the bath is called for."

"Yeah, I need to go now as well, get out of my work clothes. I'm seeing Karl later."

Fear clutched Chelsey's heart. "You won't tell him, will you?"

"What, that we've kidnapped his best mate and you and Tammy have spent the last half an hour torturing the poor man?"

Chelsey nodded, unable to respond verbally.

"No, my lips will remain sealed, as promised, even if all of this does go against my principles of fairness. Maybe that's what's wrong with the world right now, there are too many angry people filling it, like you and Tammy."

Chelsey clenched her fists but restrained herself from lashing out. "How dare you? Still, it's easy for you to say, you're not the one who has been infected with this godawful disease, are you? God help us if you ever found yourself in that position, we'd never hear the bloody end of it."

"What, like now, you mean? That's the only topic of conversation you've spoken about in days, since you went to the doctor's last week. Get a life, Chelsey, stop trying to turn the tables on others when it suits you. I've seen and heard enough around here for one day. I'm leaving, feeling physically sick, thanks to what you've done to Erik today. Don't forget that man opened up his home to us a few weeks ago, and this is the thanks he gets for showing us some kindness."

"What the actual fuck? Have you heard yourself? I seem to recall myself being a reluctant participant that night and only went along with you and Tammy because you both had the opportunity to get laid, and look how that backfired on me. You appear to be forgetting that someone *raped* me that night."

"I'm not because you're not allowing us to forget it. I know that sounds heartless but…"

Chelsey swiftly closed the gap between them and raised a clench fist and rested it against her friend's cheek. Polly ended up wedged between a chair and the patio door.

"I can't believe you said that. Call yourself a damn friend? I've had more sympathetic enemies over the years." Chelsey withdrew her fist and turned on her heel, downed the rest of her drink, then walked out of the house. At the front door, she shouted, "You're not worth it."

"Come back, Chelsey, I didn't mean it. I'm sorry. I realise I've overstepped the mark. Don't punish me like this, please, I need you guys."

"You should have thought about that before you opened your mouth. If you don't show up tomorrow, you can remove me from the contacts in your phone. The choice is yours." Chelsey slammed the door behind her and jumped in to the driver's seat of her car. She drove back into the city and drew into the Asda car park. She exited the vehicle and made her way along the footpath for a stroll by the river. It was the only way she knew of ridding herself of all her pent-up emotions, even if it was starting to rain. She raised the collar of her jacket around her neck but didn't get very far when the rain began teeming down. Within seconds, Chelsey was soaked to the skin.

"Fantastic, as if this day couldn't get any worse." She glanced at the sky and shook her fist. "Will you give me a break? What else have you got planned for me? Because I'm getting close to being at the end of my tether right now."

A fork of lightning speared its way through the black clouds to her right. It struck a small tree not thirty feet away, setting it alight. She upped her pace, scared of what might happen if she stayed out in the open in the ferocious storm. It didn't bother her that her seat would get soaked, she just needed to get home, and quickly.

Relieved to have made it back to the house before anything else major affected her, Chelsey ran through to the kitchen, discarding her clothes en route. She flicked on the kettle to make a hot drink. She tossed all her soaking-wet garments into the machine and threw in a couple of washing tabs, then set the machine on a cycle. Naked, she tore through the house and up the stairs where she ran a bath and emerged from the bathroom fifteen minutes later feeling ten times better.

After blow-drying her hair, she slipped into her velour pyjamas and went back downstairs to see what ingredients were nestled in her fridge, waiting for her to cobble together a dinner. Ten minutes later, she sat at the kitchen table, eating a mushroom omelette and baked beans. It was her go-to meal when she lacked inspiration for something nutritional to knock up.

She savoured every mouthful, her memory clouded with Erik's smug face, but when she recalled his screams, she couldn't help but smile. *I don't believe you, you fucker. You know who the rapist is. You're going to regret not divulging his dirty little secret... you've already ended up with two broken legs for your loyalty to the scumbag. I won't stop there, I promise you.*

CHAPTER 5

The following evening, the girls met up at the arranged meeting point at six-thirty, aware of Ronan's routine once he locked up the sports shop he managed in the heart of the city centre. Polly was the last to arrive. She parked her car in a spot close to the van, just in time. Her wayward behaviour was enough to get Tammy and Chelsey making plans about how they would proceed if ever she reneged on their deal.

Polly's attitude was a growing concern to Chelsey and had caused her to have a sleepless night after her run-in with her at the house the previous evening.

"She's here, finally," Tammy said once she spotted Polly parking the car.

The side door of the van slid open, and Polly popped her head in. "Hi, sorry I'm late. Not my fault, another screw-up at work that the boss expected me to sort out before I ended my shift."

"It doesn't matter, you're here now. Hop in," Chelsey ordered.

Polly climbed in and sat heavily on the seat. "There's no

need to take that tone with me. I could have easily gone straight home, but I didn't, I came here instead. You should be grateful I didn't leave you in the lurch instead of biting my bloody head off."

Tammy nudged Chelsey in the ribs, as if warning her not to get involved.

Chelsey relented, tired of arguing, and started the van. She drew away from the kerb. "You'd better get your gear on, Polly, it won't be long before we get there."

"I'm on it. Sorry to hold you up."

"And stop apologising," Chelsey snapped.

"Sorry," Polly muttered and then tutted. She removed her black hooded sweatshirt and matching jogging pants from her overnight bag and slipped them on.

Chelsey slowed the van down around twenty feet from the entrance to the gym. "If we park here, we should be out of range of the gym's cameras."

"Good thinking. That's the last thing we need, highlighting our getaway vehicle to the cops," Tammy agreed.

Chelsey kept a close eye on her wing mirror and watched several men walk through the shortcut to the gym. Each time someone came into view her heart skipped several beats. "Nope, it's not him. Hang on, this might be him. What do you think, Tammy?"

"Yes, there's no doubt in my mind that's Ronan. I nipped out at lunchtime to the sports shop to refresh my memory about what he looked like."

Chelsey sucked in a breath and let it ease out between her lips. "That was risky. Did he clock you?"

"No, not at all. I only caught a fleeting glimpse of him. He was out in the stockroom, dealing with a delivery, at least that's what one of the staff told me when I asked if he was working," Tammy replied.

Chelsey fidgeted in her seat. "On the count of three, we

get out, go to the near side. We'll make out there's something wrong with the rear tyre. Let him go past us and then make our move. Have you got the hood, Polly?"

"Yep, all ready to go."

"Are you both up for this? No hesitation, you hear me? Hit him quickly and shove him in the back of the van. It's a much busier thoroughfare than I had anticipated."

"You worry too much," Tammy said. "We've got this covered."

"Okay. Out we get, pull your hoods up." Chelsea threw open the driver's door and scooted round to the other side of the van and stood by her friends.

She kicked the back tyre and then got down to have a closer look. Then, with her hood shielding her face, she snuck a peek to see how far Ronan was from them. He was studying his phone, and she could tell he was wearing ear pods, which she suspected would work in their favour.

She stood and whispered, "Are you ready? He's distracted, this should be a breeze."

He got to within a few feet of them and glanced up, sensing there was an obstruction on the pavement ahead of him. He sidestepped closer to the grass verge and smiled. The girls let him walk past, and then Chelsea whispered, "Grab him."

Tammy clobbered him over the head with the bar. Polly screeched, and Chelsea jabbed her in the side.

"Keep the noise down, you idiot."

"Sorry," Polly mumbled.

"He's out cold. Grab his legs, I'll take his upper body. We need to get him in the van, pronto, before anyone else comes around the corner."

They grunted and heaved to get Ronan's body through the side door of the van. They managed it just in time as another man, seemingly in a hurry to get to the gym, came bounding around the corner.

The three girls retook their seats, and Chelsey slipped the van into gear and drove back to the house on the other side of the city. There, they bundled Ronan into the hallway, huffing and puffing, struggling to move the dead weight.

"Is he all right?" Tammy asked. "Did I hit him too hard?"

"You're worrying too much." Chelsey closed the door behind them. "Let's take a breather before we try and haul his arse up the stairs. Polly, is there a spare blanket around?"

"Yes, I think there's one in the back bedroom. I'll fetch it." She ran up the stairs, two at a time, and reappeared a few seconds later with the heavy blanket.

"Excellent. We'll put him on it, and it'll be easier to drag him up the stairs. Tammy and I will do the heavy lifting while you help by pushing his feet and keeping him from slipping off the material," Chelsey said.

"Sounds like a good plan to me. Tell us when you want to give it a go."

"Another couple of minutes, and then we'll start again. It was easier this time, wasn't it?"

"It went in our favour that he was distracted," Polly replied.

They all stared down at the lifeless body, and Chelsey noticed that his chest wasn't going up and down. She knelt beside him and felt for a pulse in his neck. There wasn't one. "Shit. He's not breathing."

"I told you to check him, didn't I?" Tammy shouted.

Polly screamed and instantly paced the hallway. "No, don't say that. Do something. Get him breathing again, we have to."

"How? Does anyone know how to perform CPR?"

"I learnt a while back, I had to go on a course for the gym, but I'm not sure if I can remember what to do," Tammy responded.

Chelsey clutched her arm. "You have to give it a try, you're our only hope."

Tammy sighed and sank to her knees. She placed her fingers either side of his nose and blew into his mouth. Then sat back on her heels. "Shit, I've screwed up already. I should have checked his airway was clear before I did that. What if he was chewing gum when we bashed him, and he mistakenly swallowed it and it got stuck in his throat?"

"Get your fingers in there and check," Chelsey ordered.

"Why me?"

"Because you're the only one who knows what to do," Chelsey pointed out.

Reluctantly, Tammy stuck her fingers down his throat. "It's clear."

"Now try to resuscitate him again."

Tammy held Ronan's nose and blew into his mouth and then pressed down on his chest, but it proved to be pointless. Tears ran down her cheeks. She paused, shuddered and inhaled a large breath to refill what she had expelled from her lungs. "It's too late. We don't know how long he's been dead. He might have died instantly when I belted him with the bar. I didn't think to check him. Everything happened in a rush."

Chelsey got down on the floor beside her and latched on to her arms. "None of this is your fault. It was a freak accident. Don't blame yourself."

Tammy sobbed and spluttered, "How can you sit there and say that? Flippantly say that as though his life didn't matter? It matters to me. All this is fucking screwed up. Remind me why we're doing this again?"

Chelsey closed her eyes, doing her best to calm her jangling nerves. "Because of what they did to me?"

"They? No, one person is responsible, and here we are, punishing them all, for one person's indiscretion."

Chelsey leapt to her feet and stared at Tammy. "*An indiscretion?* I've heard everything now. Who's to say he wasn't the rapist and that he wasn't the one who infected me?"

"I suppose we're never going to know now, are we? Now that he's carked it. Jesus, how has it come to this? You've turned us all into murderers."

"I haven't. Don't look at it that way. We're not murderers, we slipped up, made a genuine mistake, and he's paid the price."

Tammy jumped to her feet. "Paid the price? He's done that all right. What happens now?"

Chelsey placed her hands over her head; it was swimming. Numerous terrifying scenarios ran through her mind, making her feel as though she was spinning out of control. She glanced at Polly who hadn't said a word, and then back at Tammy and shrugged. "We'll do the test and then we're going to need to get rid of the body… tonight."

Tammy ran a hand through her hair and tugged at the roots. "Where? We hadn't made any plans for this. What are you expecting us to do, just dump his body somewhere?"

Chelsey dashed through to the kitchen and stared out of the patio door. She clenched and unclenched her fists dozens of times before Polly and Tammy joined her.

"Chelsey, you didn't answer Tammy. What are we going to do?" Polly asked.

"I don't know. I need to think this through thoroughly. This wasn't on the agenda, so no provisions were made if someone died on us. I'm not the only one here, you know. You two could come up with a solution as well as me. Why does everything always have to sit heavily on my shoulders all the time?"

Tammy flung her arms out to the sides and let them drop

against her thighs. "Because all of this was your ruddy idea. The whole kit and caboodle, and now we're in it up to our necks, God help us. None of us bargained for this, did we? Now we need to figure out what the hell we're going to do with him before we get cold feet. I can see that happening if we don't get rid of him tonight."

"Just give me five minutes to think. Why don't we make ourselves a drink, sit down and discuss this like adults?"

"Because there's a dead body lying in the hallway, and I think we should get shot of it, sooner rather than later, that's why."

Chelsey closed her eyes, blocking out her surroundings to see if that would summon up a solution to their problem. It didn't. She sank into the chair beside her and cried. "I don't know what to do for the best. Why did you have to kill him?"

Tammy punched Chelsey's arm. "Anyone would think I did this intentionally. I didn't. Now we have to deal with it, and quickly, before his skin starts to rot."

"Eeww... did you have to say that?" Polly cried.

"Shut up, both of you. It's not helping if we keep sniping at each other." Chelsey buried her head in her hands again. She tried to think of a nearby location where they could dump the body without being seen. The only saving grace in their favour was that it was getting dark now. "We need to wait until it's totally dark. In the meantime, we should put his body back in the van. And to answer your question, I haven't got a clue how long it takes for a body to start decomposing. It's not something I've bothered Googling before."

A thud sounded upstairs. "Oh great, just what we need, him getting in on the act," Tammy mumbled. "Has he been fed and watered today? Has the bucket been changed? Shit, how is he even going to get off the bed and to the bucket with two broken legs?"

"Fuck, we didn't think about that aspect when we clobbered him," Chelsey replied, deep in thought, trying to think of a solution. "We'll dump the body then come back and deal with him."

"When we clobbered him?" Tammy hissed. "No, that was all down to you."

Chelsey smiled and reminded her, "There's no *I* in team and I seem to remember you goading me on when you sat on him."

"Stop it, just stop it. All this bickering isn't getting us anywhere, is it?" Polly said. She took a swipe at both of their arms. "I'm sick of all of this, sick of you two. And most of all, I'm sick of the thought of going after the others if they end up dead like that." She pointed at the body.

Chelsey took a step towards Polly and gripped her arms. "All right, I want you to take a large breath. You're hyperventilating."

Polly gasped and shook off Chelsey's arms. "I'm fine, leave me alone, you're not a medical expert. You have no idea what my body is going through at the moment."

Chelsey inclined her head, thought it was a strange statement for Polly to make but refused to push it further when they had more important issues to deal with. Like getting rid of Ronan's body. She sniffed the air, convinced she could smell his rotting flesh. "Come on, we need to get him back in the van. I'll quickly do the test then we'll wrap him in the blanket, it'll be easier for us to carry him." Chelsey collected the kit and carried out the test.

Between them, they tugged the blanket under the corpse, rolling it from side to side when the material rucked up. Finally, with the chore completed, the three women placed themselves at regular intervals along the blanket and, on the count of three, they hoisted it off the floor. Chelsey flung the front door open and guided, what appeared to be a wrapped missile, up the garden path. She juggled the body and rested it on her thigh and awkwardly managed to open the van's back door.

"We're there. Start sliding him in. I'll hop in the back and ensure he remains covered."

Polly and Tammy heaved the weighty parcel into the van and, before long, they achieved their aim. It was time for all of them to take a breather.

"Right, jump in. I'll lock up the house, we'll come back and deal with Erik later." She shut the door, trotted up the path to the house, secured it and returned to the van. She hopped behind the steering wheel, and when she inhaled, she swore she could detect the smell of rotting flesh again. She shook her head. *I must be imagining things, it wouldn't happen this quickly, would it?*

"Where are we going?" Tammy asked.

"I think I know a suitable spot, just down the road, it shouldn't take us long," Chelsey answered.

She pulled away from the house and at the next junction, joined the main road back into Hereford, but turned off about ten minutes later when she saw the sign to Kings Caple. She'd visited the area a couple of times in the past, when an ex used to walk his greyhound out that way. She hadn't been here since she'd split up with him and hoped it hadn't changed dramatically in that short time.

"Why here? I didn't even know this place existed," Tammy asked.

"Neither did I until a few years ago. We'll have clear access to the river soon, and there's not likely to be anyone around at this time of night." She cocked an ear. The sound of running water was all around them.

"I've been here before. It's a local beauty spot. This doesn't feel right, dumping his body here," Polly piped up.

"We're doing it, end of. Get used to it, Polly."

"Pardon me for breathing. Obviously, my opinion doesn't matter, if it ever did. I'm sick of being ordered around by you, Chelsey. You're not my boss or my mother, although you act like it most of the time. I have a mind of my own, I don't need you telling me what to do twenty-four-seven."

"All right, wind your neck in. I've never ordered you around, as if I could ever do that? Sometimes I feel you need extra guidance, that's all."

"Well, I don't. So back off."

Chelsey held her hands up. "Okay, less of the squabbling. We need to get him out of the van, let's save all our strength for that. I think I saw a torch in the back of the van, we'll use that to guide our way. The bridge is a good five minutes from here." She removed the test from her pocket and swore. "It was negative."

"Shit that's just great, isn't it? And now you're expecting us to haul his arse all that way? I'm not Superwoman, you know," Tammy complained.

"I know that, but there are three of us to take the strain, not just one. We've got this. We can do it. If you'll only have faith in our abilities."

Polly and Tammy stared at each other and shrugged.

"Right, let's assume the same positions, it worked well for us last time."

Chelsey grabbed the head, Polly stood in the middle and Tammy grappled with Ronan's feet.

"I'm all set to go at this end," Tammy whispered loudly.

"All right. Nice and steady, make sure we don't overexert ourselves."

It proved to be easy enough to begin with, but as the terrain became more uneven, Chelsey wasn't the only one who was struggling to keep the body from slipping through her fingers.

"Do you want to take a break or plough on and get this done?"

"I think we should plough on. How far is it to the bridge?" Tammy asked from the rear.

Chelsey held the light up ahead of her, and in the distance, she could make out the wood and steel structure they were aiming for. "I'd say another five minutes, if that."

"Let's go for it," Tammy shouted. She rearranged the weight to get a better grip.

"I agree. I just want to get this over and done with and get out of here," Polly said.

"I hear you loud and clear. Come on, girls. Put your backs into it."

They grunted and moaned through the extra steps before they reached the edge of the bridge.

"Christ, is this thing going to take all our weight?" Tammy called out.

"We're about to find out. Let's get in the middle. We're going to have to push him through the metal uprights, they're wide enough, so I don't see it being a problem."

They stopped in the middle of the bridge.

Chelsey shifted the body into position and balanced it on the edge of the metal structure. Then she worked her way back to where Polly was standing. "On the count of three. One, two, three."

They shunted the body forward until it was hanging over the side.

Then Chelsey moved back to stand next to Tammy. "We've got this. One large shove, and he should go over the edge, no problem."

She and Tammy put in the extra effort needed, and the body made a huge splash as it tipped into the River Wye.

"I'm never going to be able to look at the Wye in the same way again," Polly whined. "I've always found it to be such a tranquil stretch of water to walk alongside at various locations throughout the county. Never again, thanks to what we've done today."

"You'll get over it. What other option did we have?" Chelsey challenged her.

"We could have buried him. I hope for your sake he doesn't get caught up in the reeds further down the river. There are some shallow parts around the bend, or had you forgotten that?"

"Fuck, now she tells us." Chelsey snarled and took a step closer to Polly.

Tammy latched on to her arm to restrain her.

"You're going to push me too far one of these days, Polly. Learn to open that trap of yours in the right places, and we won't fall out. What the hell is wrong with you?"

Polly turned on her heel and began the walk back to the van. "Nothing, you need to look in the mirror now and again and see what we have to witness every day."

"Leave it," Tammy warned. "She's not worth it."

"For fuck's sake. She can't get away with spouting crap like that and not expect me to respond, stupid bloody bitch. I'll wipe the floor with her when I get the chance, I swear I will."

"No, you won't. You're going to hold on to that temper of yours and use it against the boys, not against either of us, got that?"

Chelsey stared at her friend. "Okay, that's a deal. But someone is going to need to have a word with her, Miss Perfect, who never puts a foot wrong. She's the main reason we're in this fucking mess in the first place, because she was super keen to open her legs for Karl."

"Hey, you can't fling that at her. It was my suggestion to go back to the house with Oscar, too, or are you forgetting that?"

"No, but you're not the one who is making a song and dance out of this and keen on pointing the finger at me, *she is*. And it's getting boring now."

Chelsey drove back to the house. She opened the door as a large thud sounded above them. "What the fuck is he up to now? Polly, can you fix him a sandwich? I'll go and see what mischief he's getting up to up there."

"He can't live on sandwiches alone, he needs a decent meal inside him now and again."

"And are you going to be the one to prepare that for him?"

Polly's gaze dropped to the floor. "No. All right, you win... again."

Chelsey seethed and glanced over at Tammy for assistance.

Tammy steered Polly into the kitchen. "I'll help. Come on, the sooner we get this job completed the sooner we can get home."

Still bubbling inside, Chelsey ran up the stairs and unlocked the door to the bedroom at the front. She switched on the light to find Erik sprawled across the floor, writhing in agony. "What the fuck are you doing?"

"What does it fucking look like? You busted my legs. I need to get to the bucket to have a wee. You're going to need to help me."

She picked up the empty bucket and pulled it closer, then managed to gather enough energy to help him get back on the bed. "You'll need to hit the target from there."

"Are you crazy? I won't be able to do that. You didn't think this through properly, did you?"

"I guess I didn't. But here's the thing, I don't regret it, not a jot, you bloody moron. You had the chance to avoid all this suffering. Instead, you set out to treat me like an idiot. You thought I didn't have it in me to punish you. Go on, admit it."

He glared at her. "I put you down as a psycho the second I laid eyes on you, so did the others. Why do you think the other two got laid and not you?" He laughed.

Heat seared her veins. She crossed the room and picked up the bar on the other side by the window, the very item that had already carried out so much damage. She aimed it at his torso. His eyes widened and then narrowed.

"You wouldn't dare."

"Wrong thing to say." She slammed the bar against his ribs and immediately heard one crack.

He yelled out.

Tammy came hurtling into the room and removed the bar from her hand. "What the fuck are you doing? Don't you think he's suffered enough, Chelsey?"

"No. You didn't hear him; he was goading me. Christ, we should finish him off just like the other one."

"What other one?" Erik asked, his voice strained with pain.

Chelsey got up close and sneered. "We had the pleasure of killing Ronan and dumping his body. You should be counting yourself lucky that you're still alive. Saying that, one more smart comment from that mouth of yours and it could lead to your imminent death."

"You're lying. I don't believe you." His gaze flitted between them.

Tammy shook her head. "Unfortunately, she's telling you the truth. My advice would be to keep your trap shut if you want to get out of this situation alive."

"Actually, my friend here is wrong. The best thing for you to do is to tell me which one of you bastards raped me. That's the only way you're going to get out of here alive. And if you don't believe me, you will after tomorrow."

"What are you talking about? What are you going to do to me tomorrow?" Erik squirmed.

Chelsey rubbed her hands together until the palms heated up. "Ah, now why would I give the game away? Believe me when I tell you this, what we've put you through so far is insignificant compared to what we have in store for you. That's a promise, not just a threat. Hey, maybe you hit the mark calling me a psycho after all. I guess only time will tell if that's the truth or not. Still, you won't have long to wait, one more sleep and all will be revealed."

He gulped and faced Tammy. "You can't let her get away with this. Do something, you have to."

"Do I? You already have one dead body on your conscience, just tell her the truth and anything else we have planned for you will be a thing of the past. The choice remains with you. Don't be an idiot and keep the information to yourself, it's not going to do you any good, not in the long run. Surely you realise we mean business, by now. Why keep sitting on the information when there's no need to, why?"

"Because I'm loyal to my friends," he yelled in Tammy's face.

Polly entered the room carrying a plate and a mug of coffee. "What's going on in here? Haven't you punished him enough already?"

"No, keep out of this, Polly. He's on the verge of telling us which of his friends raped me," Chelsey shouted. She took another step closer to Erik and resisted the urge to vomit over him.

"I'm not. I told you I'm loyal to my friends. Anyway, I don't know who did it, but even if I did, I wouldn't tell you."

"Leave him alone now, let him eat," Polly insisted. She placed the plate on the bed beside Erik and tugged on

Tammy's and Chelsey's arms. "Leave him. Come on, I want to go home."

Chelsey removed her arm from Polly's clutch and then withdrew a set of shears from her jacket pocket. "You two get out of the room if you don't want to see this."

Tammy pushed an objecting Polly into the hallway and closed the door.

Erik glared at Chelsey. "You haven't got it in you. Your friends are already showing signs of rebellion, it's only a matter of time before Polly plucks up the courage to go to the cops."

Chelsey gave him one of her sinister smiles that silenced his diatribe. Before he realised what was happening, she pounced on him. He yelled out when she landed on his injured ribs. The movement knocked the wind out of his sails and allowed her the time to get hold of his hand and, in the blink of an eye, snip his little finger off. He screamed, and Tammy barged into the room again. Tammy pulled Chelsey backwards, and she landed with a thud on the floor.

"What's that for? I haven't finished with him yet."

"Oh yes you have. Look at him, he's having some kind of seizure. Shit, get your phone out and tell me what to do."

Fortunately, the Wi-Fi signal was good at the house, and Chelsey typed in the question: *How to help someone suffering from a seizure.*

Polly screamed from the doorway and then passed out.

"Shit, we'll have to deal with her in a minute," Tammy said. "Hurry up before we lose him, Chels."

"I've got it. It says to make him comfortable. Put the pillow under his head. We have to wait until the seizure has passed and then turn him on his side, make sure there's no food or drink in his mouth."

"Well, we know there isn't any. Shit, why did you have to go and do that? What has got into you? I no longer know what to expect from you. You're dangerous and out of control, Chelsey. I'm not surprised Polly passed out on us. What the fuck are you doing?"

Chelsey stood there, stunned, unable to respond.

Erik's seizure finally calmed down, and Tammy rolled him onto his side and rubbed his back as an added touch of comfort.

"I'm sorry," Chelsey mumbled.

"So you should be, but it's not me you should be apologising to, it's Erik. See to Polly, make sure she didn't bang her head on the way down."

Dazed, Chelsey checked Polly over and shook her gently whilst she called her name. "Polly, can you hear me? Come back to us, love."

It took a few minutes of coaxing for Polly to wake up. She ran a hand over her face and the back of her head. "What happened?"

"You passed out. I'm sorry I've put you through this. I'll make it up to you, I swear I will."

Polly frowned. "The only way you're going to make amends is if you let him go and put an end to this preposterous situation."

"I can't do that, and it's not fair of you to expect me to end this. I need to know the truth. Do you want the guilty party to keep sowing his oats? Infecting innocent women, like me? He gave me no choice. Someone who takes another person's ability to say no, shouldn't be allowed to roam the streets. Surely you can see that, can't you?"

"Yes and no. I admit he's in the wrong, but you're just as bad. Look at the damage you've caused already. Erik needs treatment for his injuries, which he's not going to get if you have your way, and poor Ronan is now floating down the River Wye."

"You're forgetting one important fact here."

"What's that?" Polly rubbed at her forehead.

"I didn't kill him. That was an accident, but I still didn't do it, Tammy did. So, she's as complicit as I am in all of this, but it's not her throat you're jumping down every five minutes, is it? No, it's mine."

Polly lifted her legs and tried to get to her feet with the aid of the doorframe. "You need to grow up, the pair of you. I didn't sign up for any of this, not really. I just went along with you and Tammy. I never expected things to go this far, though, despite the notes you made. I thought it was all bravado on your part. I don't know you at all. You're both evil and now you've had the audacity to burden me with some of the blame. I can't handle this. I refuse to continue and I'm revoking my permission for you to use this house as some kind of torture chamber. Neil would go apeshit if he bloody knew what was going on here."

"All right, we hear you. I agree, things have got out of hand," Tammy said.

"Okay, you win. But you're going to need to give me time to find another location suitable for our purpose," Chelsey moaned as she got to her feet.

"You've got twenty-four hours. Now, is he going to be okay to leave like this? Or should someone stay behind with him?"

"I'll do it," Chelsey volunteered. "It's the least I can do. Why don't you two get off?"

"Suits me. Are you coming, Tammy?"

"I'll be with you in a tick. You go, I'll help Chels tidy things up around here."

Polly waved and sighed. "Fine. I'll see you both soon, I hope under better circumstances."

Chelsey stared at Tammy as they listened to Polly thump her way down the stairs. "Don't say it. I know I've screwed up in more ways than one. But you weren't here, you didn't hear him goading me. He's not as innocent as he's making out."

"Hey, you haven't told us the results of his test yet?"

"It turned out to be negative, but I refuse to go easy on the bastard, not when it's obvious that he's keeping something from us, probably the truth."

"Time's running out. Don't forget we've got twenty-four hours to get out of this place before Polly makes good on her threat."

"What's she going to do? Go to the police? She's in it up to her neck as much as we are, maybe she's forgotten that."

"I'm tired. I can't think straight. Hey, he's coming around."

Erik stirred and inched his eyes open. "What happened?"

Chelsey walked over to the chest of drawers and opened the top one. She removed a pair of black knickers and returned to the bed. She wrapped the garment around Erik's hand.

He stared down at his wound and then the blood covering the quilt. "What the hell did you do?"

"You forced me to do it."

"Like shit I did. You're insane." He looked at Tammy and pleaded with her, "You've got to help me. Don't leave me alone with this bitch again. She's not right in the head, can't you see that?"

Tammy shrugged. "As far as I can see, there's an easy solution that could put an end to your sticky situation. Tell her the truth, and your suffering could be over just like that." She clicked her fingers.

"Never."

Tammy nodded and made her way to the door. "If that's your decision, you might want to say a few prayers tonight, before you fall asleep."

Chelsey chuckled and left the room with Tammy. They high-fived each other in the hallway, ran down the stairs and out through the front door. Tammy drove the van back to the lockup, and Chelsey changed her mind about staying at the house. Instead, she headed back into the city but made a detour en route.

She knocked on the door of the small, terraced home. Polly opened the door. She licked the food off her fingers and appeared shocked to see Chelsey standing there.

"Oh, hi. Did I forget something at the house?"

"No, I wanted to check on you, make sure everything is all right between us. Can I come in for a chat?"

"I'm expecting Karl in ten minutes, I'd rather he didn't see you here."

"Fine by me. I'll be gone before then."

She held the door open, and Chelsey followed her into the hallway. Polly turned to smile. It slipped when she saw the bar raised above Chelsey's head.

"What the…?"

The bar fell, knocking Polly out cold. Chelsey turned off all the lights and prayed that Karl didn't have a spare key. He knocked on the front door a few minutes later, earlier than anticipated. By this time, Chelsey had dragged Polly into the lounge, just in case he peeked through the letterbox to see where she was. Polly's mobile had rung constantly since he'd arrived. Chelsey hid by the curtain and watched him drive away.

Once he'd driven off, all she had to do was bide her time and wait until the neighbours were all tucked up in bed before she dragged Polly's body out to her car. That was as far ahead as she'd thought…

CHAPTER 6

Sara was travelling into work when the call came in. "DI Sara Ramsey, how may I help?"

"Morning, ma'am. I've been requested by the pathologist, Lorraine Dixon, to give you a call."

"Bummer, this early in the morning? That doesn't bode well. Okay, tell me where I should be heading, and I'll turn the car around before you tell me the rest."

"Kings Caple, do you know it?"

"I've heard of it. Do you have a postcode for me?" Sara indicated and pulled into the side of the road. The woman on control gave her the information which she entered into the satnav. "Just turning around now. Can you give me any other details?"

"A body was found in the river."

"Don't tell me, by a dog walker, right?"

The woman laughed. "Correct. The man rang nine-nine-nine at a little after six-thirty this morning. The pathologist attended the scene straight away."

"Thanks, if you can get in touch with her, tell her I'll be fifteen minutes at the most."

"Will do. Thank you, ma'am. Have a good day."

"I'll try." Sara ended the call and switched on the radio. She tapped her fingers to an old Lionel Ritchie song that whiled away a few minutes of her journey.

When she arrived, there was no mistaking that she'd come to the right place. Two SOCO vans and a patrol car were parked in a gravel area close to the common. Sara togged up in her protective suit but left off her shoe covers until she got to the scene. She signed the log at the cordon and ducked under the tape.

"Ah, good morning. I'm glad you came. I wasn't sure if you'd be dealing with a case or not at present. I took a punt you'd be free. Are you?"

"No, but that's never stopped me from showing up at a scene before, has it? We're working a missing person case at the moment, so there's definitely room for another case to run alongside it. Are we looking at foul play or a suicide?"

"The body is wrapped in a blanket that got snagged on the reeds. A dog walker, you know, the infamous one?" Lorraine laughed at her own joke. "Anyway, he found the body in between the bank and the reeds."

"Lucky the body wasn't washed downstream; we've had a fair amount of rain lately. Male or female?"

"Male. Fairly young. The good news is that I have some ID on him."

"Wow, that's got to be a first. It'll make both our lives easier, won't it?"

"You'd think so. Walk this way."

"If I did that, I'd get arrested."

"The old ones are the best." Lorraine groaned.

"Have I ever let you down on that front before? It's all I know."

Lorraine shook her head.

"I'm just going to inform Carla where I am, she'll only

worry if I don't show up on time, given my current personal circumstances."

Lorraine frowned.

"Mark had his operation yesterday. I dropped by to see him last night, but he slept through my visit. I didn't bother staying long."

"Shit. I had no idea. How did it go?"

"The consultant seems to think he'll make a full recovery. We'll see."

"I'll keep my fingers crossed. Such a young age to get it."

"Apparently, the doctor suggested it might have been caused when Mark was playing football for the youth team. He got hit in the nuts a few times. Who knew it could lead to this?"

Lorraine raised her hand. "I did. If only people realised."

Sara tutted and turned her back to make the call. "It's me. I am at work, just not at the station. I'm out at Kings Caple. Lorraine and her team have fished a body wrapped in a blanket out of the river."

"Bugger. Do you want me to join you? Are we going to be taking the case on as well as the missing person one?"

"Yes, we can split the team in two. It's not like we're getting very far with the other case, are we?"

"True. Okay, I'll have a quick word with the team, ensure they know how to proceed with the *miss per* and then join you, if that's what you want?"

"You read my mind. See you soon."

She walked towards Lorraine, slipped her shoe covers over her boots and stared down at the victim. "Any idea how he was killed? Was he dead before he entered the water or did he drown?"

"Initial indications are that he received a whack to the head. I'm assuming it was harder than intended and probably killed him."

"So, the killer panicked, wrapped him in a blanket and thought they'd throw him in the river."

"I think you've probably hit the nail on the head." Lorraine collected an evidence bag from the bank off to the right. "His ID."

Sara fought with her protective suit to locate her jacket pocket and withdrew her notebook. She jotted down his details. "I'll call the station, see if he's been listed as a missing person." She made the call and had it confirmed within a few minutes. "Apparently, he was due to meet his girlfriend for dinner last night, after he went to the gym. He didn't show up. She tried to contact him and got worried when he neglected to answer his mobile, so she rang the police."

"At least that gives you a timeline to work with. This place is out of the way so was probably chosen for a reason."

"I can't see one person being able to handle his body, can you?"

"Hard to say. You mentioned he usually visited a gym. Maybe he had a run-in with someone down there, a muscle-bound goon who whacked him too hard, shoved him in his vehicle and drove him miles away to get rid of the body."

"That's quite a vivid imagination you have there, Lorraine, have you been practising?"

"Cheeky cow. Here's the dog walker's information, you'll be needing that for his statement."

"Blimey, you're being super-efficient today, what gives?"

Lorraine frowned. "I'm always efficient, it's my middle name."

Sara coughed and said into her fist, "Amongst others."

Lorraine took a swipe at her arm, but Sara managed to dodge it.

Sara grinned. "Anything else I should know?"

"I think that's it. It's pretty cut and dried, I'd say, wouldn't you?"

"Not really, the victim is far from dry."

Lorraine tutted. "I think it was time you were leaving."

"I can't, I need to wait for Carla to get here."

Lorraine pointed behind her. "She's arrived. Which is a relief for all of us."

"Charming. That's the thanks I get for showing up at a scene early, before I've even clocked in at work."

"Not as early as some of us, just saying. Enjoy the rest of your day."

"I doubt if that will happen," she mumbled, knowing what lay ahead of her—sharing the devastating news with the victim's loved ones. "Morning, Carla. Don't get comfortable, we're off."

"You mean I could have prevented wasting a suit?"

"Them's the breaks. We have more important chores to cover."

"Can I at least take a look at the body now I've come this far?"

Sara stepped back and gestured for her partner to squeeze past her.

"Heck, he's quite young. Intentional?"

"That's what we believe. Let's see if we can fill in the blanks with the next of kin."

"You have his ID?"

Sara waved her notebook. "I have. I'll arrange for a uniformed officer to get a statement from the dog walker when I get back to the car, just in case I forget later."

"Hey, you haven't told me, how did Mark get on yesterday?"

"He was still out of it when I visited him on the ward last night. The consultant seems to think they got all the cancer and that he should make a full recovery."

Carla slapped a hand over her chest. "Thank God for that. You must be so relieved."

"I am. Hopefully we'll have happier times ahead of us. Saying that, his mum is still not faring too well."

"Shit, there's always something to put a damper on things, isn't there?"

"It's called life. What doesn't break us, always leaves an imprint on us somewhere along the line."

"Ain't that the truth?"

They returned to the cars, stripped off their suits and deposited them in the black sack next to the cordon. Before she got in her vehicle, Sara contacted the desk sergeant and gave him the details of the dog walker. He assured her he'd send a constable out to the address ASAP.

"Follow me?" Sara asked Carla.

"Of course."

THEY PULLED up outside a semi-detached house on one of the older estates on the edge of the city. Sara noticed a woman with long blonde hair standing at the window. She waved at the woman and walked up the small concrete path. On either side of the path, the lawn had been removed and replaced with slate. Dotted around were half a dozen tubs with spring bulbs emerging through the winter pansies.

Carla joined her at the door just as it was opened by the woman.

"Are you from the police? They told me to expect someone, but I didn't think you would show up this early. Or have you found him?"

"Sorry, I didn't get your name?" Sara kicked herself for not asking who had logged the victim as missing.

"It's Lindsay Dillon."

"Can I call you Lindsay?"

"Yes. Just tell me, have you found him?"

"I think it would be better if we went inside to discuss the matter."

Lindsay slapped a hand on either side of her face. "Oh God, you have, haven't you? I can see it in your eyes. It's not good news, is it?"

Sara took a step forward, forcing the woman to back into the hallway.

Lindsay gripped the banister with both hands, her knuckles stretching until the colour faded from them.

"Why don't we take a seat in the lounge?" Sara suggested.

Lindsay turned and staggered into the room on the left.

Sara faced Carla and rolled her eyes. "This is going to be a tough one," she mouthed.

Carla nodded her agreement. "I'll make a drink, if she wants one."

"Thanks."

They followed Lindsay into the lounge. She was sitting on the sofa, a tissue wrapped around her fingers.

"I've been dreading you showing up. I've had a terrible pain in the pit of my stomach all night. Please tell me, don't hold back, I need to hear the truth."

Sara and Carla sat in the armchairs opposite Lindsay.

Sara sighed. "I'm sorry, you're right, the news isn't good. Is there someone we can call to come and sit with you?"

Tears bulged, and Lindsay shook her head. "No, we have no one in the area. We moved up here a few years ago, for work. We visit my family during the holiday. Ronan lost both of his parents to cancer, when he was in his teens. He was an only child and has no other living relatives as far as he was aware. Where did you find him?"

"In the river."

"Oh God. He couldn't swim. Did he fall in? Is that what you're telling me?"

"Unfortunately, we believe he was put there deliberately."

"I don't understand."

"After I spoke with the pathologist at the scene, she believes Ronan was struck on the head with a heavy object. It was enough to kill him. The killer then wrapped his body in a blanket and threw him in the river. He got caught up in the reeds, otherwise his body might have drifted for miles."

"I can't believe I'm hearing this. Do you know who attacked him?"

"Not at this stage. No evidence was found at the scene. The station informed me that you registered him as a missing person last night. Can you tell us when you last saw him or had any contact with him? I take it you lived together?"

"That's right. I was working late at the office. I usually give him a call as soon as I get home. I tried, but his phone kept ringing, and then eventually his voicemail kicked in."

"Where did he work?"

"In the city. He was a manager at Go Sports in town."

Sara glanced sideways at Carla to see if she knew of the shop. Her partner nodded.

"I saw him in the morning, made him aware that I was going to be late. He made arrangements to go to the gym after work. Some weeks he goes two or three times, so it was nothing unusual. We planned to meet up after. I booked a table for seven-thirty at Miller and Carter. I was there, but he failed to arrive. I rang the gym, and they told me he hadn't shown up for his slot with the instructor. None of this is making any sense to me."

"Which gym was it?" Sara asked.

"Weights and Measure."

"We'll get in touch with them. Did he walk to the gym or take the car?"

"No, he left his car at home. It's the BMW outside. He usually took a shortcut up the alley." She got out of her seat and pointed out of the window. "It's just there. He was at the gym within five minutes. Handy having it just around the corner." She sat again and pulled another tissue from the box next to her and blew her nose. "I can't believe I'll never see him again. We were talking about getting engaged in the summer. We wanted to wait until we were both more settled in our jobs before we committed to getting married. Now all that will remain a pipe dream. How am I ever going to cope without him? This house will be full of memories which is going to make it hard to deal with and, no, I don't want to sell it, I can't because the market sucks at the moment with the high interest rates. I fear I'm going to be in negative equity. Sorry, I shouldn't be thinking ahead like that, it's what I do. I'm a party organiser for large corporations."

"Ah, it's okay, you don't have to make excuses to us. You're a practical person, there's nothing wrong with that. Can you tell us if Ronan had fallen out with anyone recently?"

Her head dipped. "No, I don't think so. If he had, he didn't tell me. Are you saying that someone he knew would most likely have killed him?"

"No, not necessarily. It's the first question we ask people. We're searching for any relevant background information that will help us build a case. Is there anything you can think of?"

"No. He more or less kept himself to himself, we both do. He spent most of his time with me, went out with his friends occasionally but not that often. He worked hard and was entitled to let off steam now and again. He went to the gym when I worked late. Do you think he had a run-in with someone down at the gym?"

"We'll make a point of asking the manager when we see him. Has Ronan mentioned if he's had any problems at work lately? Perhaps he's sacked someone in the last month or so?"

"No, he made a point of always treating his staff fairly. They've all been with him since he took over as manager there, which is unusual—ask any manager who takes on a new role. Adjustments in staffing levels often take place as soon as a new manager is promoted. Not this time. Everyone got on well with Ronan, he was fair-minded and always willing to listen to his staff's concerns, large or small. It's how he gained their respect so quickly."

"He sounded like a nice man. You mentioned his friends. We'd like to speak with them, if you can give us their details?"

Lindsay chewed on her lip. "I'm not sure I can, you know how lazy we get when we have mobiles. All his contacts were in his phone."

"I understand. Their names will do, we can carry out the necessary research from there."

"Let me think. Umm… there's only one or two I can remember. Karl Payne, with a K not a C. I recall his name because my brother is called Carl, spelt differently, and my friend is Shelley Payne. I've heard him talk about Oscar before but I'm sorry, I can't give you his surname."

"Don't worry. Any idea where Karl works?"

"Gosh, now you're testing me. I believe he works at an electrical place."

"Selling or fitting?"

Lindsay nodded. "Definitely selling. I think it's to the trade, not to the general public if that helps. Maybe try Thomson's Electrical."

"That's great, we'll give it a try. I think we've covered everything now. Are there any questions you'd like to ask us?"

Lindsay paused to think for a moment or two. "Umm… I'm not sure if I want to do this or not but will I have to identify his body?"

"Yes, I'll pass your information on to the pathologist. She'll be in touch with you once the post-mortem has been carried out."

"Oh no, the thought of him having to be cut open... how awful."

"I'm afraid it's the law when a death is considered suspicious. He'll be sewn up when you see him," Sara added.

"I'm glad to hear it." Lindsay wiped a tear from her eye and rose from the sofa. "I'll show you out. Will you promise me you'll do your best to find out who did this to him?"

"As with any case we investigate, my team and I always give it our all. We won't let you down."

"Thank you, that means a lot to me. It's the not knowing that will probably eat away at me."

"Don't worry. Try to take things easy today. Again, we're truly sorry for your loss."

They left the house and returned to their cars.

"Where to now, back to the station?" Carla asked.

"No, I'm going to pay the gym a visit. See how close he got to the premises. They're bound to have cameras on site. If it's at the end of the alley, there's every chance the cameras picked up the attack on him."

"Unless it happened off camera, in the alley."

Sara pulled a face and chewed her lip. "Possibly. Why don't you head back to the station? Look up the electrical firm Karl works for; Lindsay didn't seem too sure she had the right name. I'll meet you back there. I shouldn't be too long."

"Rightio. Want me to check out his social media? See if I can find out anything further from that?"

"Excellent idea."

They went their separate ways at the end of the estate. Within minutes, Sara drew into a spot outside the gym. She noted how many cameras were covering the site and then entered the reception area. The gym was virtually empty, and the girl sitting at the desk was filing her nails and chewing on a piece of gum.

Sara showed her warrant card. "Is the manager around?"

"Nope, he's nipped out for five minutes. Can I help?"

"I'll wait, thanks."

"Suit yourself. He'll probably be longer, he's not the best timekeeper in the world."

Sara smiled and took a seat in the grey padded easy chair close to the door. There were a bunch of fitness magazines on the table. She picked one up and flicked through it, pausing now and again to admire the models in their skimpy shorts, showing off their pecs and six-packs, or was that twelve-packs in some cases?

A muscular man in his early thirties entered the main door around ten minutes later.

The receptionist pointed at Sara. "The police are here to see you, Warren."

"Thanks. Hi, I'm Warren, the manager. Would you like to come through to my office?"

"Why not? I'm Detective Inspector Sara Ramsey."

"Has Dani offered you a drink?"

"No, but it's fine. I shouldn't take up too much of your time, I'll get one back at the station."

He showed her into his office and offered her a seat. "What can I do for you, Inspector Ramsey?"

"I'm investigating a serious crime, and we've been told the victim was a regular at your gym."

"He or she?"

"Male. Ronan Finch, do you know him?"

"Ah, yes. I took the call from his girlfriend last night; she sounded very worried over the phone. He had a trainer booked and didn't show up. I told her the same thing. Therefore, I don't think I can be of any help to you."

"That's a shame. He was definitely on his way here, and as he only lives around the corner it's puzzling what could have happened to him in that time."

"I hear what you're saying. I knew he used to take the cut-through down the footpath, if it helps. I know his home is down that way and that he used the gym because it was convenient."

"I was wondering if I could view any footage you have from your cameras from last night."

"Be my guest, anything to help the police with their enquiries. Why don't we relocate to the other office? That's where the security equipment is."

"Fantastic, thanks very much."

They nipped next door, and he selected a disc from the pile. "This is yesterday's recording. I change it first thing in the morning."

"That's good to hear."

"What time shall I search for? Wait, she rang me at about seven-thirty, so it would have been somewhere between six and six-thirty," he said, answering his own question.

Sara smiled and watched the screen as he whizzed through the disc. He stopped at six, but there was nothing to be seen. He pressed Forward and paused again at six-thirty. A blue van drew up outside the car park, which raised her suspicions. The driver got out of the van and disappeared out of view. They reappeared a few minutes later, started up the van and drove off. Sara noted there was a passenger in the front, next to the driver. "That's odd, they drew up and left a few minutes later. Can you take a copy of that section for me?"

"Of course. What are you thinking?"

"I couldn't possibly say at this stage. Ronan didn't appear up until that time, but the van blocked the view of the camera—was that intentional? What did the driver do when he or she got out of the van?"

"I can't deny, it did seem strange. It won't take me a second to run a copy off for you."

Sara kept her eyes on the screen, in particular the driver of the van.

Warren made the copy and handed Sara the plastic case.

"Would you mind playing the disc a little more, just in case Ronan appears?"

Warren nodded and continued to play the recording. They saw a man jog out of the alley and run towards the gym entrance.

"That's Mick Greenwood, he's here most nights."

"Do you have a contact number for him? It might be worth me having a chat with him. There's something going on with that van that doesn't sit comfortably with me, it was blocking our view. Maybe he saw something as he exited the alley."

"Possibly. I'll have to get his details from the system, but we'll need to go back next door, to my office. Are you finished with the recording?"

"I think so. Thanks."

He led the way back into his office and sat behind his desk. After tapping away at his keyboard, he wrote down a phone number and an address for Mick Greenwood. "Here you go. Is there anything else I can get for you?"

Sara picked up the sheet of paper and stared at it. "No, this will do nicely. I appreciate all the help you've given me this morning."

"My pleasure. I hope you solve the crime and Ronan shows up soon."

Sara rose from her chair and walked towards the door. "Sadly, he's already been found. We believe he's been murdered."

Warren stared at her and then fell back in his chair. "Hell, I had no idea. He was a good man, from what I can remember. Eager to keep his fitness levels up. Can I ask how he died?"

"A whack to the head before he was thrown into the river."

"Shit. I remember him telling me once that he enjoyed all forms of fitness but failed to see the benefits of swimming as he couldn't swim, something he and I had in common. I loathe it. My father threw me in the pool when I was four, expected me to know what to do. I didn't. Luckily, there was a lifeguard on duty, and he came to my rescue. Mum was furious with my father, and our family was never the same after that day. My parents got divorced six months later. I've always felt guilty about that."

"Nonsense, it wasn't your fault. The onus should lie with your father. That was an irresponsible and nasty thing for him to do."

"I realise that now, but the guilt remained with me for years. I never saw him again; he didn't bother visiting me after Mum kicked him out of the house. I heard a few years later that he had committed suicide, drank himself to death is how the coroner put it."

Sara wagged her finger from side to side. "That wasn't down to you, he was at fault, not you."

"Thanks, I try to tell myself that, but it's not always easy to deal with."

"Maybe you should have a word with a counsellor. It might be worth a shot, to rid you of your demons."

"Not for me. I tend to deal with personal issues in my own way. I'll get there, one day. Nice meeting you. Don't hesitate to come back if you have any further questions or fancy a discount on a gym membership. Our female client list is growing year on year."

"I can imagine. I'd love to take you up on that offer, but my schedule isn't usually nine to five, in fact, it's anything but."

"It's there for when you need it. I might even drop a note down the station, offering a ten percent discount to all the officers. Always on the lookout to boost our members. It might be the initiative they need."

"It can't do any harm, especially if you mention my name. One good turn deserves another. Nice meeting you, Warren."

He beamed. "And you, Inspector Ramsey. I hope you solve the investigation soon."

"Me, too."

Sara left the gym and made her way over to where the van was parked on the recording. She searched the ground for clues, but the area was clear. "What happened to you, Ronan?"

"First sign of madness, talking to yourself like that," a female said as she jogged past.

"Don't I know it?" Sara called after her, and they both laughed.

She went back to her car and contacted Carla at the station. "I've got a sighting of a blue van parked outside the gym, covering the cut-through. Might be something or it might not. How are you getting on?"

"I've checked the social media. Ronan appeared to have a lot of friends who often commented on his posts. Umm… one name in particular is standing out."

"And that is?"

"A Karl Payne. I've looked at his profile, and he works at Thomson's Electrical. It's fairly close to the gym. Might be worth you stopping by if you're in the vicinity."

"I'll do that now. Do you have a postcode for me?"

Carla gave her the details, and Sara punched them into the satnav.

"Creepy, yes, it's two streets away. I might even walk there. I could do with some extra exercise. Being at the gym has given me a guilt complex."

"Rather you than me. Give me a shout if you need me. I'll keep trawling my way through the SM accounts of the victim, see if anything else stands out."

"Okay, I shouldn't be too long. I'll drop by the baker's on the way back. Get a list of requirements from everyone and text it to me."

"Will do. Good luck."

Sara ended the call, tucked her phone into her jacket pocket and set off. She arrived at Thomson's Electrical on the nearby trading estate around five minutes later, thankful that it hadn't rained. That thought hadn't entered her mind when she'd told Carla of her intentions. Her phone jangled in her pocket. She removed it and saw a text from Carla with the team's requests for lunch.

Shoving her phone back into her pocket, she entered the showroom. A young man was standing behind the counter, staring at his computer screen. Sara had to cough to gain his attention.

"Oops, sorry. I didn't see you come in."

"Don't apologise, I can see you were engrossed in your work."

"Checking through a customer's order before I sign it off, ready for delivery. Can you give me two seconds to complete it?"

"Sure. Don't mind me." She picked up a trade magazine off the counter and flicked through it. Got bored within seconds and replaced it. By that time, the young man was ready to assist her. She showed her warrant card. "I'm DI Ramsey. Is it possible to speak with Karl Payne?"

"Karl?" He grinned. "Oh no, has he been a naughty boy?"

Sara smiled. "No, at least I don't think he has. I'm making

general enquiries and would appreciate a quick word with him, if he's available?"

"He's in the warehouse, dealing with this order. He should be free soon, once he's secured the box and put it on the van."

"I'll take a seat and wait for him."

"I'll let him know you're here. Help yourself to a drink from the vending machine. Here's a token to use, save you paying."

"You're too kind. Thanks. It's been a while since I've had a coffee." She chose a white latte with one sugar from the machine and sat on the low padded seats in the corner, fearing she'd struggle to get to her feet again once the time came. She sipped at her drink whilst flicking through yet another boring trade magazine of electrical components and was halfway through her coffee when another young man appeared at her side.

"Hi, I'm Karl Payne. Stuart told me that you're from the police and you want to see me."

"That's right. Is there somewhere else we can go?"

"Only the canteen. It's a tip in there, but at least we'll have some privacy. Have I done something wrong?"

"No, you haven't. Umm... if I can only get out of this damn chair..."

He offered her his hand.

She accepted it and pulled herself to her feet. "Do your chairs often eat your customers?"

He laughed and showed her through a door that led to the rear of the building. "Excuse the mess. The cleaner walked out at the end of last week, don't ask me why." He chortled.

"I think that's self-explanatory, don't you?"

"I'd ask you to take a seat, but they're just as mucky. It's cleaner over there, by the window."

"Suits me."

They repositioned themselves in the relatively clean area.

Sara inhaled a breath and said, "Umm... I'm afraid I've got some bad news for you, concerning a friend of yours."

He frowned and cocked his head. "And who might that be?"

"Ronan Finch."

He slumped against the wall. "What about him?"

"His body was pulled out of the river this morning."

He ran a hand through his ginger hair and shook his head over and over. "I can't believe what you're telling me. But he couldn't swim."

"We believe he was probably knocked unconscious and died from his injuries. His fully clothed body was then disposed of in the river out near Kings Caple. Do you know that area?"

"No, should I...? Sorry, I shouldn't have snapped at you. I've heard of the area, but I don't think I've ever been out that way. Sod it, I can't get my head around this. Someone clobbered him, do you know why?"

"I was hoping you'd be able to fill in some of the blanks for me."

He pointed a thumb at his chest. "Me? How... would I know? This is the first I'm hearing about it. Are you accusing me of bashing my friend and getting rid of his body?"

Sara raised her hand. "I'm going to need you to calm down. That's not what I said. I'm not blaming you. What I need to know is if you were aware if Ronan had any problems leading up to his death."

"Wait, how did you know he was my friend?"

"Through his social media accounts. Sorry, I should have said. Did you know him well?"

"Yes, we were best of friends. I still can't believe this, and no, he didn't have any issues with anyone, not as far as I'm aware of." He stared at the floor.

"What about his home life, was everything good there?"

"Yes. Lindsay and Ronan were meant for each other. Oh God, does she know about this?"

"I had to break the news to her earlier."

"Should I go round to see her, lend her my support? I don't really know her that well but I'm still willing to lend a hand. They haven't been in the area long."

"She told us. Maybe leave it a day or two. I'm sure she'll be happy to see you once the news has sunk in. She's going to need to identify his body in the next day or two; she might need someone to go with her, for support."

"Oh yes, I could do that. I'd be happy to. She shouldn't have to do that horrible job alone."

"Always better if the person has support. Can you tell me when you last saw Ronan?"

"A couple of days ago. We went out to the pub on Sunday together, just for a quick pint at lunchtime, then I went back to his house. Lindsay had cooked a roast dinner for us. I had to tell Mum not to bother cooking for me. I live with my parents and fancied a change. The offer was on the table, so I jumped at the chance."

"Did Ronan ever confide in you?"

"All the time. He didn't tell me he was having any issues with anyone. I would have offered to have helped him, if he had."

"How did he seem on Sunday?"

"Fine. We both were. We only stayed at the pub for about an hour. We were looking forward to our lunch and watching the match on the TV afterwards. Lindsay left us to it, she's not really into football. She nipped next door to her friend's house."

"Did he tell you he was going to the gym yesterday?"

"Yes, he goes a couple of times a week. He was trying to persuade me to sign up, but I've tried it before and detested having to stick to a routine. Why did you mention the gym?"

"Because Lindsay told us he was due to have a session there last night, but his instructor said he didn't show up."

"That's strange. I've never known him to let anyone down in the past, he's genuinely the most reliable guy I know. Or should I say knew. That's hard, talking in the past tense."

Sara smiled. "It'll get easier. I'm sorry for your loss. If you can think of anything that will help my team solve the investigation, now would be a good time to tell me."

He turned his back on her and placed his head against the wall. He bashed it a few times until Sara touched his arm. He stopped and whispered, "Why him? I can't believe he's gone."

"Don't punish yourself like this. I promise you, I will get to the bottom of this."

"Will you? How can you when you're here asking me all these questions? It's obvious that you don't have any evidence as to who is responsible for his death. Where do you begin?"

"By talking to family and friends who knew him well. Don't give up on me so soon. The truth will come out in the end, and we will find the person responsible for his death."

"Then what?" he asked, a note of bitterness in his tone.

She frowned, and he faced her once more.

"Then, we'll arrest the person and put them before a judge. It'll be up to the jury to convict the killer, but again, we'll be reliant on the information we obtain from Ronan's friends and family. Was he close to anyone else?"

"Yes, a few others. We used to go out together once a month."

Sara removed her notebook from her pocket. "It would help if you gave me their names."

"I doubt if they'll be able to tell you any more than I can, I was his closest friend."

She smiled, hoping to prise the information out of him

without the need to become heavy-handed. "It would still be good to have a chat with the others."

Karl ran a hand around his face. "Can I get back to you later with the information? I don't like handing out personal details without checking with the people concerned first."

"Of course. I'll give you my card. Ring me once you've spoken to them. Is there anything you'd like to tell me before I leave?"

"No. Forgive me if you think I'm putting unnecessary obstacles in your way. Past experience tells me not to divulge details without checking with the person, giving me the all-clear."

What a strange thing to say. "It's no problem. My team will probably have the necessary details for me when I get back to the station anyway, they're still going through Ronan's social media accounts. If you can get back to me either later today or first thing in the morning at the latest."

"I'll do that. Nice to meet you."

"And you. I must get off. You've got my number. I look forward to hearing from you soon."

"You will, you have my word."

He showed her back to the main entrance.

Sara cursed when she saw it had started raining. "Just my luck."

"I wish I had an umbrella I could offer you, but they're just not my thing. Are you parked up the road?"

"A few streets away at the gym. I'll be fine. Thankfully, I had the foresight to wear low heels today, I'll jog back." She shook his hand. "Call me ASAP, if you will?"

"I'll do that."

She bolted out of the door and kept to the side of the street that was tree-lined in the hope the branches would shield her from the worst of the weather. When she reached the car, she removed her coat and shook off the excess drops then threw it on the back seat.

In her haste to get back to the station, she forgot to stop off at the baker's. "Sorry, guys. Craig, can you nip out and pick up some sandwiches?"

"On my way. What's everyone having?"

Carla picked up her mobile. "Allow me. I'll text you the list."

Sara gave her the thumbs-up and removed her jacket which she placed on the back of a chair and put in front of the radiator in her office.

Carla appeared in the doorway. "I have a few things we need to discuss, when you're ready."

Sara walked towards her. "I'm all yours. What's up?"

"I'm hoping you won't shout at me when I share the first snippet of information."

Sara closed her eyes and sighed. "I'm waiting."

"Err... you might have a press conference to attend at three this afternoon."

"Oh, is that right? And pray tell me who arranged that for me?"

Carla grinned. "Jane Donaldson rang to speak to you after she heard about the victim who was found in the river and said she had a slot free for this afternoon if it was needed. I took the liberty of taking her up on her offer. Did I do the wrong thing?"

"No, not this time. I hope my hair dries before then, the journalists will think we've sunk to new depths, getting drowned rats to address the public."

"I doubt it. You'll be fine. You can always shove your head under the drier if push comes to shove."

"Great, then I'll look like Crystal Tipps."

"Who?"

"It doesn't matter, it's probably before your time, and mine come to that. Look it up on YouTube."

Carla went back to her desk and opened up her phone. She laughed constantly for the next couple of minutes.

"Piss off. How did you get on with the SM accounts?" Sara asked.

"Hit and miss."

"Don't worry about it, I've got Karl Payne calling me back later with a list of friends. He's just got to get the all-clear from them first."

Carla's nose wrinkled. "He what?"

"It's fine. He told me that he'd overstepped the mark in the past and was erring on the side of caution. We have to accept his decision, but it can't prevent us from checking out his social media, which you've already done."

"I can keep checking the other accounts, X and Tik Tok, see what they throw up. I've only concentrated my efforts on Facebook and Instagram so far."

"Yes, do it. I'll be in my office dealing with the post and then making a few notes for the conference. Will you bring my sandwich in when Craig gets back?"

"Consider it done, and sorry about the conference. Between us, we thought we were doing the right thing."

"No apologies necessary, and you did. It still doesn't prevent my stomach churning at the thought of facing all those journalists. You know how worked up I get before being thrust in front of them."

Carla smiled. "I'd volunteer to take over the task for you but... I'm up to my neck in researching the different social media accounts of the victim."

Sara rolled her eyes and walked away. "Nice swerve. Laters."

. . .

THE CONFERENCE WENT SURPRISINGLY WELL, in the end. Sara was far more prepared than she thought she would be. The journalists bombarded her with questions she couldn't answer due to either lack of evidence found at the scene or the fact that the background information she had about Ronan Finch was yet to be discovered. Up until now, Karl Payne hadn't got back to her. The conference was due to be aired on the evening news. Craig being Craig, had agreed to man the phones until ten that evening. Sara dipped into the petty cash tin and gave him a tenner to order a pizza.

"Call me if anything interesting comes in, won't you?"

"I will, boss. Enjoy your evening."

During the afternoon, Sara had tried on several occasions, time permitting, to call Mick Greenwood, but his phone appeared to be turned off. Undeterred, she called him one last time on the drive home.

"Hello."

"Ah, Mr Greenwood, finally. Sorry to disturb your evening. I'm DI Sara Ramsey. Do you have a moment to answer a few questions for me?"

"The police? Yes, what's this about?"

"A possible incident that happened outside the gym where you train which occurred last night."

"Incident? I don't recall seeing any incident."

"You did attend the gym, though?"

"Yes, that's right. But I still didn't see an incident."

"Did you notice a blue van parked on the side of the road after you left the small cut-through just outside the gym?"

He paused to think for a moment. "Yes, that's right. I didn't think anything of it at the time. There were three people outside the van, all wearing hoods. One of them appeared to be checking the tyre. It seemed okay to me, but perhaps they discovered a nail in it or something. After I passed them, they all jumped back into the van, and it sped off, tyres squealing, that sort of thing."

"Interesting, thank you. Yes, I viewed the footage from the gym and caught sight of the van but didn't see three people because of the camera angle. I only saw the driver and a passenger sitting next to them. Could you make out anything else about these people?"

"No, sorry. I'm not the nosey type. Don't stick my beak in where it's not wanted, if you get what I mean?"

"I do. Can you give me some indication of their build perhaps?"

"Hard to say when someone is down on their haunches."

"I know. Okay, thanks so much for your help. I really appreciate you accepting my call. Enjoy the rest of your evening, Mr Greenwood."

"You, too."

Sara ended the call and turned down the next road on her right that led her to the hospital car park. She collected the ticket at the barrier and parked in the first available space she could find.

She left the car and ran up the slight incline to the main entrance. The lift took a while to arrive, and when it did it was nearly full. She stepped aside to let the people out before she got in. She pressed level two and closed her eyes, willing the old thing to get her to her destination without any unnecessary mishaps along the way.

Mark was sitting up in bed when she got there. He appeared to be very pale but seemed pleased to see her when she leaned over and kissed him on the lips.

She touched his face and asked, "How are you tonight?"

"Sore down below. I had to ask for extra painkillers earlier, but other than that I'm fine. All the better for seeing you. How are you?"

"Tired but glad to see you're faring better." She sat in the chair next to his bed and held his hand. "Sorry, I forgot to pick up something from the shop. I was in such a rush to get here to see you."

"You're all I need. I'd probably sit here and flick grapes around at the other patients if you'd brought me some."

She slapped his wrist. "Naughty you. Have they told you when you can come home?"

"Not for a few days yet. I'm comfortable enough, don't worry about me, love."

"But I do worry. Still, at least you're in the best place, getting some much-needed rest. You've been working flat out for months and dealing with your mum's illness as well, it's bound to take its toll."

"Have you found the time to ring Dad, to see how Mum is?"

"Yes, she's exhausted but resting when she can. He didn't seem overly concerned about her, it's what the doctor told him to expect before she was released from hospital. So, you need to stop worrying about her and concentrate on getting better yourself. Your dad told me he was going to ring the hospital today to see how you were. Did he?"

"Yes, the nurse told me he'd called. As if he hasn't got enough to worry about, he's also keeping me in his thoughts. I feel guilty about that."

"You're nuts. Of course he's thinking of you. Your mum would be too, if she knew. We all care about you very much, love. Have you slept much during the day?"

"Yes, mostly this morning, but I also had a quick nap this afternoon, because I wanted to be fully alert when you came in this evening."

"And here you are, bright as a button. Let me know if you're getting tired, all right?"

"You'll soon find out, when I drop off while you're talking."

Sara laughed. "Nothing new there then."

They shared another kiss, and she noticed him wince a little.

She squeezed his hand. "Try not to exert yourself too much."

"I would hardly call leaning over to kiss my wife exerting myself."

"You know what I mean. Have you eaten?"

"Yes." He lowered his voice and whispered, "The food in here isn't up to my exacting standards."

She chuckled. "I bet."

"Are you still working that missing person case?"

"That's right, but now we've taken on a second case, a murder investigation."

"Ouch, are you sure you're not taking on too much?"

"I discussed it with the team, and they're of the same opinion as me, that we can handle both. Unfortunately, we haven't discovered anything worth chasing on either case, so far."

"You will, you and your team are tenacious, you always get your man." He rested his head back on the pillow and closed his eyes.

Sara remained with him a further ten minutes, listening to his gentle snoring, relieved to see that he appeared to be on the mend, then she kissed him on the forehead and left for the evening. The nurse behind the desk smiled as she approached.

"He seems fine, tired but otherwise okay. Or is that all a front? How is he really doing?"

"He's doing well. Proceeding as planned. You'll have him home in a few days if he continues to improve. Will you be taking time off work to care for him?"

"Gosh, it's not something we have spoken about. How long will his recuperation be?"

"It varies from patient to patient, around six to eight weeks."

"Ouch, he's going to hate that."

"A necessary evil, he's had a major operation."

"I know. However, it's not me you have to convince, it's him. I'll see what I can do at work, have a word with my boss."

"He told me you're an inspector with the police. That's a tough job. I admire you."

"It's nothing really. I round up the bad guys and put them away behind bars. You're the one who has the toughest role to contend with."

"Not really. Most of the patients are as well-behaved as Mark, but that can turn on a sixpence."

"I can imagine. I still admire the work you do. Where would the NHS be without committed staff such as yourself?"

The nurse nodded and answered the phone as it rang beside her. She waved at Sara and paid the caller her full attention. Sara left the ward and took the stairs down to the reception area. She walked out of the building, paid her parking fee and returned to the car.

Driving home, the weariness overwhelmed her. Misty greeted her at the front door. She bent down and swept her up in her arms and snuggled into her fur. "Have you missed me, sweetie?"

She removed her jacket and shoes and went through to the kitchen to feed Misty. Before she topped up her bowls, she let her four-legged companion in the garden. With that chore completed, she knocked up an omelette for herself and settled down in the lounge to catch the end of the news. Sadly, she missed the press conference that must have aired earlier.

Without realising it, Sara fell asleep on the sofa. The sound of her mobile ringing woke her up. "Hello?"

"Sorry, did I wake you, boss? It's Craig."

"I must have dropped off. Any news?"

"Nothing. Just checking in with you before I head home for the evening."

"You're a good man. Come in at midday tomorrow, okay?"

"I'll be here at nine as usual. You worry too much."

"What can I say? I'm a born worrier. Goodnight, Craig. Thanks for putting in the extra hours."

"Always a pleasure, and I got a free pizza thrown into the bargain, too."

They both laughed, and Sara ended the call. She secured the house, and Misty followed her upstairs to bed. She lacked the energy to have a shower so instead removed her clothes, put them over the chair, and the last thing she remembered was laying her head on the pillow and pulling Misty in for a cuddle.

CHAPTER 7

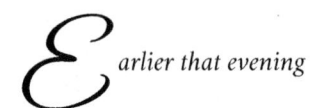

Earlier that evening

"It's a shame Polly has decided to take a back seat," Tammy said.

"Have you heard from her?" Chelsey asked. She drove the van to the location and tried to keep the apprehension out of her tone.

"I've called her several times. I think she's ignoring me. I won't bother for a while. She's upset, you know how much she likes to sulk."

"Don't I just? Are you all right continuing with the plan, just the two of us?"

"Why not? We're the ones who did most of the work when we abducted the others, so it suits me."

"Good. I think we should hit them all quickly. We'll pick up Karl tonight, maybe hit Oscar tomorrow. Will you be all right with that? I know you're seeing him."

Tammy waved her hand to dismiss the notion. "I'm fine. Needs must."

They had both agreed to knock off work early to get the job done, now that they were a body light with Polly going AWOL. Chelsey felt bad keeping the news from Tammy about holding Polly hostage. But her hands were tied. She feared what Polly was capable of doing. She had been teetering on the edge of the abyss for a while, but killing Ronan and getting rid of his body in the river had tipped the scales in the wrong direction for Chelsey's liking, forcing her to act before Polly's conscience kicked in and got them all in trouble.

Chelsey slotted into a space at the edge of the car park. The main entrance to the showroom was still lit up, and there were two cars left on site.

"I'm taking a chance that he'll be the one who locks up."

"And if he's not?"

"Then we'll follow him and force him off the road if we have to. This must happen this evening, without fail."

They sat in silence as Karl left the building with another man. Karl locked the door while his colleague made his way towards his vehicle. He drove away and waved at Karl as he exited the car park.

"This is it. I'm going to draw up alongside him. Get ready to jump out. Have you got the bar handy?"

"I have. I promise not to hit him as hard as I hit Ronan."

"Make sure you don't. I haven't got the strength to dispose of yet another body so soon."

"All right, there's no need to go on about my mistake."

"I wasn't. Hang tight, here we go." Chelsey reversed the van and then drove into the car park.

Karl paused beside his vehicle and smiled at them. "Can I help? We're closed until the morning now."

Tammy jumped out and swiped at him with the bar. He

fell to the ground but was still conscious. Chelsey left her seat and joined her friend. She removed the bar from Tammy and bashed Karl over the head again. He fell backwards, knocked out cold.

"Christ, you told me not to hit him too hard, and yet you've bashed the living daylights out of him."

"Don't exaggerate. Grab his legs, and we'll toss him in the back."

They huffed and puffed and, with an extra effort from both of them, they successfully managed to wrestle his limp body into the rear of the van.

"Let's get out of here." Chelsey switched on the radio and drove back to the cottage. She pulled up outside the cottage just as the news came on. "Shh... listen. Shit, that means we have to work quickly. Are you up for collecting Oscar tonight instead of tomorrow?"

"What the hell? If we have to. We'd better dump Karl first. Secure him in the house and then make a move."

"You read my mind. Do you know where Oscar is this evening?"

Tammy racked her brains. "I think he's finishing a car, a favour for a friend. Once we've got Karl upstairs, I can give him a call, see how long he's going to be, if you want?"

"Sounds good to me."

Chelsey opened the front door and collected the blanket they used to transfer the bodies from room to room.

"It's going to be a struggle getting him up the stairs with only the two of us," Tammy said. "Just getting him in the van zapped my strength, and you're expecting us to abduct Oscar as well, tonight?"

"Dig deep, it'll be worth it in the end."

"For whom?" Tammy bit back.

"Don't start. Let's get him inside before someone drives past."

"We're as remote as we can get out here, no one is going to pass us."

"There's always a first time."

They dragged Karl's body from the back of the van. He landed on the blanket with a thud. Then, between them, they staggered up the path and into the house.

Tammy dropped the blanket and gasped for breath. Hands on her hips, she doubled over and panted wildly. "Jesus, this is ridiculous. We're never going to be able to drag him up the stairs. It was bad enough when there were three of us, it's an impossible chore with one less."

"All right. I agree. We're going to have to keep him downstairs instead. Lounge or dining room?"

"Who cares? Either one is fine by me."

"Dining room it is then. If we both drag the blanket from this end, it'll be easier on our backs."

And it was, thankfully. Job completed, Tammy rang Oscar, her voice taut with anxiety. Chelsey stood beside her, urging her to smile so it would transfer to her voice.

"Hi, love. What time do you think you'll finish tonight?"

"I'm under the cosh to get it ready tonight for Steve, he's travelling to Manchester tomorrow. I suppose I'll be finished about nine. Why? What are you up to this evening?"

"I thought I'd drop by to see you. I have a surprise for you."

"You wouldn't be trying to distract me, would you?"

"Me? How would I be able to do that?"

"By being in the same room as me."

"I promise not to distract you for too long. I need to get an early night."

"Hmm... that sounds good to me. Shame I won't be there to join you. Drop by when you want."

"Naughty. I'll see you in a little while."

"You can count on it."

Tammy blew him a kiss and then ended the call. She collapsed into a heap on the floor and rocked back and forward. "Hell. How the heck did we get into all of this?"

"Don't start doubting what we're doing now, Tammy. We've got a few days left, and then the truth will be revealed. Please, I need you, don't let me down now. Polly has already ditched the cause. If you do it as well then all we've done so far will be for nothing. I wouldn't be able to live with that, would you?"

"Okay, you've convinced me. Can we get on with it?"

"I've got to feed Erik, check if he's all right, and then we'll head off again."

"I'll boil the kettle, make him a drink. We need to tie Karl up again before we leave. What are you going to feed him?"

"I bought a few sandwiches the other day and put them in the fridge, they should still be in date. If they're not, tough shit. He's lucky we're feeding him at all."

Tammy smirked. "You're a harsh woman when crossed. Remind me not to get on your bad side."

"Wise words, make sure you stick to them. Hey, I'm a pussycat compared to some women who have been wronged over the years."

"I'll take your word for that, you've obviously carried out your research on the subject."

"I have. Let's get this show on the road."

Erik kicked up a fuss when they delivered his food and drink. Complained that his wounds were hurting him, but his whingeing fell on deaf ears.

"Don't worry, you'll soon have all your friends around you."

His brow furrowed. "What are you talking about? I heard you downstairs. Who was with you?"

Chelsey placed a finger on her chin and smiled. "That

would be telling. Eat, drink and be merry, because everything as you know it will be changing soon."

"I'm tired of you issuing me with threats." He sneered. "Just get this over with, kill me and be done with it. You've made my life a misery these last few days, you might as well put an end to it."

Tammy remained by the door. "Chelsey, let's go. Leave him."

"In a minute. He deserves to know what lies ahead of him. If it wasn't for him and what he did that night, my life wouldn't have changed forever." She crossed the room and picked up the bar then menacingly walked towards him.

Erik squirmed and scooted back on the bed, wincing with every inch he moved. "Don't do this. Not unless you're going to end it. My body can't stand any more. I'm a broken man in more ways than one, and that's down to you."

Chelsey crept forward, her adrenaline pumping fast. Until Tammy warned her again.

"Leave him, Chels. Time is marching on. We need to go now."

She grinned, and their gazes locked for what seemed like an eternity.

"Chelsey, don't do this."

"Listen to Tammy, she's talking sense," Erik pleaded.

Chelsey revelled in the power she had over him but then backed away and returned the bar close to the window again. "Saved by the bell, so to speak. Needs must, we have a very important appointment to keep, which kind of lets you off the hook… for now."

"Thank you," Erik whispered. He released the breath he'd been holding.

Chelsey spun on her heel and sauntered sexily towards the door. She closed the door behind her, and she and Tammy chuckled.

"You really enjoy putting the fear of God into him, don't you?" Tammy said.

Chelsey walked the length of the hallway and down the stairs. "You could say that," she called over her shoulder once she'd reached the bottom.

THE GARAGE DOORS were closed when they arrived. Chelsey slammed the heel of her hands against the steering wheel. "Damn, I thought it would be open."

"Not at this time of night. Hey, he keeps the little door on the right open."

"Phew, that's a relief. We're going to need to keep our balaclavas on until we get back to the house, all right?"

"Absolutely. I wouldn't have it any other way. I'm ready when you are, I think. Although, I wish this wasn't happening, not to Oscar. I've grown quite fond of him lately."

"How fond?" Chelsey asked warily. She hoped she wasn't getting into another fraught situation like they'd had with Polly, she knew how that had panned out. Another nightmare scenario added to the mix that she could have done without.

"Just fond. Come on, let's get in there before I change my mind."

Chelsey nodded and pulled on the balaclava. She fiddled with it, ensuring it was in the right position for her to see and to be able to breathe properly, then waited for Tammy to give her the thumbs-up that she was ready. It came a few seconds later. Chelsey opened the door and pressed herself against the side of the vehicle. Tammy joined her. The forecourt was lit up, and it was situated on a main thoroughfare in to the city. The odd car drove past, now that the rush hour had died down.

"Are there any security cameras on site?"

"I think so. It shouldn't matter, not with us dressed like this and the numberplate removed from the van."

"I agree, everything is covered in that respect. Just remember to keep the balaclava on at all times. If he struggles and manages to whip it off one of us, we must keep our heads down until we can put it on again, got that?"

"Makes sense. Come on, we need to get in there before I get cold feet."

Change my mind, get cold feet... that's the second time in as many minutes you've virtually said the same thing. You're not exactly filling me with confidence about what lies ahead of us.

Tammy nudged her in the ribs. "What's the delay?"

"Nothing, I'm going over things in my mind. All done now, let's make this happen."

They each carried a bar towards the small doorway.

Chelsey eased the door open and peered through the gap between the hinges to get an idea of where Oscar was in relation to the entrance. "He's on the far side, in the inspection pit beneath the car. This is going to be tricky. Do you know if there is a panic alarm in the garage?"

"I don't think so. If there is, he's never mentioned it to me. Shit, now you've got me freaking out."

"Don't, that's the last thing we need."

Chelsey crept through the doorway and hid behind the stock-filled metal racking that was opposite and gave her a good view of Oscar's movements. She beckoned for Tammy to join her. She closed the gap quickly and stood behind Chelsey. "We need to get closer without alerting him, but how?"

"You're the one with all the answers, I'm just tagging along for the ride."

"What the fuck?" Chelsey seethed.

Laughter filled Tammy's eyes. "I'm teasing. However, I

can't think of another way of getting closer without alerting him that we're here."

"Great. We're going to present ourselves as the aggressors then, in the hope that he'll be too scared to react."

"If you say so. I'll follow your lead. What if he recognises my voice?"

"You're going to need to disguise it. Talk deeply and aggressively, that should put him off the scent, for now."

"Okay. I'm ready when you are."

Chelsey spent the next few minutes observing Oscar work in the pit beneath the car. He reached for the odd spanner or piece of equipment now and again, but most of the time he was focused on the job in hand. She counted backwards from three on her fingers. On one, they broke cover and ran towards their target.

"Get out of the pit. Do it."

"What the fuck? Who are you? What do you want?"

"Enough questions, get up here, now."

Oscar ascended the set of concrete steps to join them with his hands raised above his head. "What is this? I haven't got anything of value here. You're making a mistake."

"Shut up. I want you to speak only when I ask you a question, got that?"

"Yes. I'm sorry. I don't want any trouble, that's the last thing I need."

"Shut up! We're going to walk outside to our vehicle. You're going to get in to the back. Any fuss, and these bars will damage your skull, do you understand?"

"No. I mean yes. I understand your instructions, but why? Are you kidnapping me?"

"Give the man a gold star. Five for effort. That's our intention. We can either do this the hard way or the easy way, the choice, as they say, is yours."

"I don't want any trouble. I'm willing to go along with

your plan but I fear you've got the wrong person. If you intend to kidnap me in the hope of getting paid a ransom, you're going to be disappointed. My family aren't wealthy. I don't own this place outright, it's only rented. I haven't even got my own home; I live with my parents and sometimes stay overnight with my girlfriend."

"What did I tell you about keeping quiet?"

"I'm sorry. I'm nervous. I always talk a lot when I'm scared."

Chelsey ran at him, the bar raised threateningly above her head. "Shut the fuck up!"

"Consider it done. I'm sorry," he mumbled, followed by a large gulp.

"We're going to leave now." She nudged him towards the door that had remained open.

"I should lock up first, the key is in the office."

"Leave it. We'll switch off the lights and close the door behind us."

"But what if someone breaks in and robs me of all my equipment? I won't be able to trade."

"Do I look bothered?"

"Err... I can't tell, you're wearing a mask."

Chelsey rolled her eyes. "You're pushing your luck," she said in a gruff voice that was by now putting a strain on her throat. She shoved him in the back, towards the door, and looked over her shoulder at Tammy who had got into step behind her.

They reached outside just as a lorry came around the bend. They got caught in its main beam. The driver honked his horn at them but carried on going.

"He might get on the radio and call the police," Tammy whispered behind her.

"There's every possibility. Let's make this quick. Close the door behind you."

She shoved Oscar in the back and ordered, "Move it. Any more delays, and I'll batter you until you're black and blue, and believe me, I'm not one to dish out idle threats."

"I believe you. I've done everything you've asked of me so far. Please don't hurt me."

Tammy closed the door to the garage and ran ahead of them to open the rear doors to the van.

"Get in." Chelsey clattered the bar against his back, hitting him between the shoulder blades.

"I'm doing it."

Once Oscar was inside and seated in the chair, Tammy tied his wrists together and put some gaffer tape over his mouth.

"Is that going to be enough to keep him from bothering us during the trip? I have my doubts."

"Is it, Oscar? Because I can knock you out with my trusted friend if not."

His eyes widened, and he nodded.

"Good, then this will do." Chelsey hopped out of the van. Sirens wailed in the distance. "Let's get out of here before they arrive, if they're heading our way."

She and Tammy jumped into the front seats, and Chelsey drove off. In her mirror, a police car rounded the corner and screeched to a halt on the forecourt of the garage.

"That was a close one," Tammy said. "You'd better put your foot down in case they spot us."

"Within reason. Let's go nice and steady, without drawing attention to ourselves."

Tammy kept her eye on the mirror to her left and in between threw a cursory glance in the back to check on how her fella was doing.

Chelsey was less frantic in her actions. She drove back to the house, drew up outside and leapt out. She flung open the back door, startling Oscar. Tammy joined her a few seconds later. Together, they untied him and moved him into the house. This was a much more civilised way of dealing with their captives.

Chelsey led the way up the stairs with Oscar compliant and sandwiched between her and Tammy.

"Who's out there? Please help me, they've been holding me for days. I'm injured… get help," Erik shouted as they marched past his room.

"I recognise that voice. Erik, is that you, mate?" Oscar shouted.

"Oscar, is that you? I'm in here, get help. They'll be back soon."

"They're here, mate. They've just kidnapped me. What's all this about?"

"Stop talking. Now move," Chelsey ordered and gave him an extra shove to get him moving again.

Chelsey steered him into the final room at the end of the hallway, far enough from Erik that they wouldn't be able to hold a conversation, although she knew the odds of that happening were very slim once they were left alone.

Tammy had collected a bottle of orange juice and a sandwich from the fridge. She placed it on the bed beside Oscar while Chelsey secured his legs and arms in front of him, allowing him to eat.

Then they left the room. Once the door was shut, he immediately started calling out to Erik.

Chelsey stormed back into the room and raised the bar. "Do I have to use this?"

"No, I'm sorry. I won't cry out again, I promise. Don't hurt me."

"Make sure you don't. Keep it shut, and we're going to get along famously. One last thing, I need to take a sample from you."

"A what?"

She produced one of the HIV tests and ordered him to open his mouth. Reluctantly, he obliged, and she ran the swab around his gums, top and bottom.

"What's that for?" he dared to ask.

"That's for me to know. Get some rest. Any noise, and Bertie Bar will bash your skull in, am I making myself clear?"

"Yes, you won't hear another peep out of me."

Chelsey left the room again, and she and Tammy removed their balaclavas then made their way back down the stairs where they watched the test results appear.

It was negative, much to Tammy's relief. "Jesus, can't we let him go now?"

"No, that's out of the question. I've had enough for today. We'll check on Karl before we leave."

"What about doing a test on him?"

"I was going to wait until he was awake, but yes, it makes sense to do it while he's out cold. Let me get another test from the kitchen, I bought some extra ones. How are you feeling about Oscar being here?"

"Not happy, especially now his result has put him in the clear. I'm worried that he knows Erik is here. He must be wondering what the hell is going on."

"I'm sure Erik will fill him in after we leave."

Tammy sucked in a breath. "Shit, that means he'll also tell him who is behind the kidnappings."

Chelsey shrugged. "It is what it is." She unlocked the dining room door and turned on the light. Karl was in the same position they'd left him in. "Help me sit him upright, so I can gain access to his mouth."

They pulled him into position, and Chelsey ran the swab around his gums then put the test aside while they lowered Karl to the floor again.

They secured the room once more.

"Should I put some food and drink in there for him, in case he wakes up?"

"Might be an idea," Chelsey agreed. She set the test on the table and waited for the lines to appear.

Tammy removed another sandwich and orange juice from the fridge. "We'll have to bring some more tomorrow, there's only one left."

"I'll sort it."

Tammy delivered the drink and food and then rejoined Chelsey in the kitchen. They stared at the test for the next ten minutes until they got the answer they were waiting for. Again, it was negative.

"Bugger. That leaves us with one more person to try. It has to be Daniel."

Tammy chewed her lip then said, "And if Daniel's test is negative, we're screwed."

Chelsey ran the different options through her head and shrugged. "I haven't thought that far ahead of me."

"What? I can't believe what I'm hearing."

Chelsey rose from her seat. "We should get going. Are you up for jumping Daniel tomorrow night, after work?"

"If there's no other way around this, yes, with an added caveat that I think you need to really consider what we do next, when you get back home this evening."

"I will, I promise. Are we ready to rock and roll?"

CHELSEY ARRIVED home to find Polly sitting upright in her chair, her hair messed up, the tape securing her mouth doing its job of keeping her quiet. Chelsey hadn't intended to be gone so long, and there were signs that her friend had soiled herself.

"Sorry. That's the one and only time I'm going to apologise to you. You shouldn't have gone against us. The Three Amigos, remember?" She tore the tape off Polly's mouth.

"Ouch, bitch. I don't know who you are any more. Why keep me locked up here, like this?"

"Because I thought you were going to dob us in to the police. I had to prevent you from taking that route."

"You're treating me like one of the boys, punishing me for something I haven't done. Does Tammy know that you're holding me here?"

Chelsey shook her head.

"I thought not. She'd be livid if she knew. You've seriously lost the plot and you need help, Chelsey. If you let me go, I can help you to arrange that, if that's what you want?"

"I don't, all I want is justice. We have one more lad to pick up now before the truth comes out."

"And what then? Have you thought about that? What are you going to do with me? Keep me here, trussed up like a prisoner in Guantanamo Bay, for eternity? I want to go home. I don't think you've thought this through properly, have you?"

Chelsey's head sank low. "You're right, I haven't. My head has been all over the place. All I wanted was to punish the boys, prevent what happened to me occurring again."

"I understand that, but you've gone about it the wrong way. Why abduct me and keep me tied up like this, why?"

Chelsey paced the floor in front of her friend. "Because I feared you were going to go to the police. I'm sorry, I regret my actions, I truly do."

"Are you going to let me go now?"

"I can't. I still don't trust you enough."

"What the fuck? You're not thinking straight, this is insane to treat me like this. Please, I'm begging you, let me go. I promise I won't go to the police."

"I can't. You've given me nothing but gyp the last few days, don't you think I'm under enough pressure as it is?"

"Let me ease that burden on your shoulders. Free me, and I'll sit down with you. We can make this work if you'll let me go."

Chelsey struggled to believe her. "Forgive me if I don't. I have trust issues nowadays that are hard to set aside. I'm sure you can understand that, can't you?"

"But... but I'm pregnant."

Chelsey stopped pacing and faced her. She shook her head in disgust. "You're unbelievable. Is this true? Or are you trying to trick me?"

"It's the truth, I swear it. Untie me before you harm the baby."

Chelsey's eyelashes fluttered closed. She hoped that blocking out the fear in Polly's eyes would make the situation bearable. It didn't. "I can't deal with this, not on top of everything else. How could you be so irresponsible, knowing what those men were like and what they'd done to me?"

"You're pathetic if you believe I did this intentionally."

"Does Karl know?"

"No. I only found out myself a few days ago. I was trying to find the right time to tell him. I'll do that when I see him."

"He's at the house," Chelsey mumbled.

"What? You've got him? Have you hurt him?"

"No, he's safe. I told you, we only have another one to pick up now."

"This is going too far, no, correct that, it's already gone too far. Has Tammy asked where I am?"

"I've told her you asked to be left alone for a few days."

"And she accepted that?"

"Yes. She knew you were teetering on the edge, struggling with what was going on around you." Chelsey raised her arms in defeat and dropped them. "I don't know what to do for the best now."

"You can start by letting me go. I need to go to the loo, it's not good for the baby if I hold on all the time. You've left me alone all day, I'm desperate now, and some food would be good, too. Can you fix me something to eat?"

"Yes, of course I can. I can't let you go, though. I'll fetch a bucket, you can use that."

"What? I can't. I refuse to, you can't make me."

"I can. It's that or nothing, the choice is yours."

The floodgates opened, and Polly rocked in her chair. "You used to be my best friend, and yet here you are, treating me like a sworn enemy. How did it come to this?"

A lump appeared in Chelsey's throat. Polly was right. They used to be so close, and now she was here as her captive, and pregnant with Karl's child to boot.

Chelsey sat in a chair opposite Polly and reached for her hand. "I wish I could trust you, I really do."

"You can, I swear I would never go against you, ever. Won't you give me another chance, Chels? I miss being with you and Tammy. I know it's only been a few days, but you treating me this way... is there any way back for us? Or have I ruined everything that was ever good between us?"

"I'm torn. I miss what we once had but I'm also determined to see the plan through to its conclusion. I can't do that if I'm distracted. And you, my dear friend, would be an unwanted distraction. I would be forever looking over my shoulder, wondering—no, waiting—for the police to show up, because I truly believe that if I were to set you free, you'd go to the police station right away. Tell me I'm wrong."

Polly swallowed hard and glanced to her left. "I wouldn't. How can you sit there and think that of me?"

"You're a born liar, trying to fool me into believing you have Tammy's and my best interests at heart. You haven't. If I untied you, gave you your freedom back, at the first opportunity you'd either go to the house, set the boys free, or venture down the cop shop and tell them about our plan. Go on, admit it. I'm right, aren't I?"

"How can you sit there and accuse me of such callous behaviour? What you're basically telling me is that our twenty-plus years of friendship mean absolutely nothing to you."

Chelsey sat back and let her friend's comment sink in for a while. "Do you want to use the bucket or not?"

"Is that it? Are you going to ignore everything I've just said to you? Purposefully putting our friendship on the line?"

Chelsey stood and stared at Polly. She pointed at her chest. "Me? I think you're deluded if you believe I'm to blame for the deterioration in our relationship. Nothing could be further from the truth. You're the one who got cold feet about our agreement, not me."

"I didn't. It's your assumption I did. I did nothing wrong, or have you conveniently forgotten that part?"

"I'm bored with this conversation. Use the bucket or don't, see if I care. I'm going to fix us something to eat. Don't expect a lot, I detest spending time in the kitchen. Will pasta do you? I sometimes have it with beans and grated cheese."

"It sounds horrendous, I'd rather starve to death. Now leave me. I'll use the bucket, but only if you leave the room."

"Fine. Can you manage?"

"Get out, Chelsey, stop pretending you give a damn!"

She left the room to do some thinking of her own. In the kitchen, while she knocked up her meal, she switched on the TV to watch the news and saw the female detective, Inspector Ramsey, pleading with the public to come forward with any information they may have about the van that a witness had seen parked outside the gym the night Ronan Finch went missing. That disastrous evening seemed a lifetime away. This week had happened in a blink of an eye. Now they had three men secured at the house and only one more to pick up. That would take place tomorrow. The dilemma Chelsey had was with the van, it had been identified as a vehicle of interest to the police.

Do we risk using it one final time or use a different vehicle instead?

CHAPTER 8

Sara drove into work, her mood angrier than the clouds overhead.

How could we have missed it? Something so obvious should have struck us immediately. But we're all guilty of failing to see what was right in front of us all along.

She flew through the reception area, gave a cursory wave to the desk sergeant who was deep in conversation with a member of the public and ran up the stairs two at a time, her heart pumping wildly.

The rest of the team were already there, thanks to the traffic jam she'd managed to get caught up in. Leaving the house five minutes late had severely impacted her day, but it had also allowed her the time to sit and contemplate the cases they were working on.

"Gather around, folks. Carla, would you mind making me a coffee? I'm in dire need of one this morning."

Carla leapt out of her seat, obviously wary of the tone Sara had used to issue her request. "Here you are. Is everything all right?" she whispered as she handed Sara her drink.

"No. Far from it. Take a seat." Sara blew on her coffee,

using the exercise as a distraction to calm herself. She was livid, getting herself more and more worked up because of what she needed to do next. Rarely, during her lengthy time in the Force, had she had to reprimand her team, but that was about to change.

The other members of her team fidgeted in their seats, seemingly nervous about what she was going to say next.

The few sips of coffee Sara managed to take before she opened her mouth appeared to have the desired effect of calming her, if only slightly. She ran a hand across her face. She glanced at her partner and saw the worried concern etched into her features.

She blew out the stale breath she'd been holding in for longer than was necessary, and her gaze drifted over each team member. "It grieves me to say this, but you guys have let me down. Not just a little bit but by a huge amount."

"What?" Carla asked.

Sara silenced her with a raised hand. "Let me finish, Sergeant Jameson. All week we've been working two cases, separately. All right, let me correct myself there, one case slightly less than the other, but you get what I mean. Me, I believe I have had good reason for possibly taking my eye off the ball, what with my husband having surgery for a life-threatening condition, however, there's no excuse for you guys to let me down so badly."

"Now wait just a minute," Carla said. She stood and began walking towards Sara.

"Sit down, Carla. Let me finish what needs to be said. You'll get your chance for a rebuttal afterwards."

Carla returned to her seat and folded her arms.

Sara could tell how angry her partner was, but it was nothing compared to how she was feeling. She ploughed on, regardless. "In all our years working together, I can't recall this ever happening. Missing a clue that has been sitting under our noses all week long. To say I'm disappointed in all of you is an understatement." She wandered over to the whiteboard and circled the word 'van' under the first victim and again on the other side of the board under the second person's name, Ronan Finch.

"Shit," a male voice muttered.

She turned to see Craig's head drop. Suddenly, she felt sorry for him. Wondered if she was overreacting, reprimanding her team like this. She had never found herself in this situation before. Sara took another couple of sips from her coffee, which again went some way towards calming her. "Is there something on your mind, Craig, that you wish to share with your colleagues?"

"No, but I do have an apology to make, boss. To you. I should have been the one to have made the connection. I'm the one who sits here for hours on end trawling through CCTV footage and tracking cars through the ANPR system. This mishap, if you can call it that, is down to me, no one else."

Sara shook her head. "I dispute that but thank you for being man enough to own up. The clues were there for all of us to see, and it bypassed each and every one of us, not just you."

"What did?" Carla shouted, her tone sounding more and more irate. "Why can't you just come right out and tell us how we've screwed up, instead of expecting us to work it out for ourselves?"

Sara raised an eyebrow. "Well, I'm glad to see at least one member of my team is on the ball. I've given you a clue, Carla, are you telling me you still haven't grasped what the connection is?"

Carla squirmed in her seat, and her gaze coasted between Sara and the word she'd circled on the board. "Bugger. Okay, my fault. I'm sorry. Guilty as charged for not seeing it the first time round. We've all been busy doing other things, though. It takes a while for us to carry out the important background checks and, in my case, I spent all day going through Finch's social media accounts. I assure you, that in itself has been a mind-numbing experience."

"I accept that, but this one significant clue should have at least been picked up by one of us. I'm including myself in this screw-up as well, despite what I'm going through. We're all guilty of not seeing what was obvious. Now we have to make amends for this major cock-up."

"How?" Carla asked.

"I know how. We need to track down that van, and quickly," Craig admitted.

The phone rang in Sara's office. She ran to answer it. "DI Sara Ramsey."

"Sorry to trouble you, Inspector, it's Jeff on reception. I was hoping to catch you on your way through, but I got caught up helping a member of the public with their problem."

"These things happen. What was it you wanted to speak to me about, Jeff? Sorry if I appear rude, but can you make it snappy? I'm in the middle of my morning meeting with the team and we've reached a crucial point."

"Oh, yes, of course. There are two things really. The first is, I received a call not long after I clocked in, from a distraught woman wanting to report her son as missing. The other is that I had a note left on my desk telling me that a lorry driver had seen something suspicious going on at the garage on the A49 towards Callow."

"Something suspicious? Can you tell me more?"

"He was driving at the speed limit, which is quite fast on that stretch of the road. He came around the corner and caught two figures carrying weapons of some sort, pushing a man in overalls. The driver said that it looked like they had come out of the garage and were heading towards a van."

"Interesting. Was the man being abducted perhaps?"

"The driver admitted that was his first thought."

"Did he give any further information about the van?"

"Only that it was dark blue. The driver turned his lorry around, but by the time he drove back to the garage the van was gone. He waited on site for a patrol car to show up. The officers checked the premises and found the door open, but no one was inside. When I came in this morning, the first thing I did was try to contact the person we have listed as the keyholder, but his phone is ringing out all the time."

"Damn. Okay, I'll send one of my guys over in a while, see what they can find. Thanks, Jeff. Wait, the missing person, can you give me the name?"

"Sorry, yes, I forgot to tell you. It's Karl Payne."

"Double crap. We only went to question him yesterday. Thanks, Jeff. I'll get back to you if I need anything else. Who filed the report?"

"His mother. He lives with her and failed to come home at his usual time. She's tried to contact him, but his phone is ringing out, as well."

"The plot thickens. Wait, what's the name of the keyholder at the garage?"

"Oscar Nelson, ma'am."

"Cheers, Jeff." She ended the call and returned to the incident room to address her team once more. "I've just had a word with the desk sergeant. He informed me about two incidents that we should be aware of. The first is that Karl Payne has been reported missing." Her gaze landed on Carla whose eyes had widened upon hearing the news. "And the second piece of information he had for me was that a blue van was seen, possibly abducting a man, out at the garage near Callow. The desk sergeant has tried to contact the keyholder, Oscar Nelson, but hasn't been able to get through to him."

"Fuck," Carla muttered. "I should have said something sooner."

Sara rolled her eyes. "About what?"

"It was getting late yesterday when I found a thread on Ronan's Facebook page that gained plenty of attention from his friends. I was in the process of going through all the likes that post obtained. I've got a list on the go here somewhere, and both those names are on it. I'm aware that Karl and he were friends, but Oscar's name is new to us. Umm... I also wrote down Erik Pittman's name..."

"You what? And you never thought to mention it before we finished our shift yesterday?" Sara kicked out at a nearby chair, sending it scuttling across the floor until it slammed into the wall.

"I'm sorry. It was a long day. I had every intention of picking up where I left off first thing this morning. I was going to run it past you once I'd carried out some extra research."

"Un-fucking-believable... I have no words other than that. Jesus, do I have to do everything myself around here?"

"That's grossly unfair," Carla challenged.

Sara walked towards her, locking eye contact with her partner. "Is it?"

Carla glanced down at her desk and waved the list she had generated. "It's all here, but first I just wanted to make sure what I was telling you had some credence. It's the way we've always worked in the past, why should this case be any different?"

Sara glared at her and then turned and walked into her office, slamming the door behind her. She needed the space to cool down and the view of the Brecon Beacons helped her to do that. However, she remained in her office, sifting through her mail for the next thirty minutes. Once her anger had subsided to a minimal level, she returned to the incident room and approached Carla. "Can I see this list of yours?"

Carla handed it over without hesitation.

There were a dozen names on the list. "Have you searched all the names?"

"I've just finished. I found an interesting photo on Oscar Nelson's page of five men on a night out together. He was pictured with Ronan, Karl, Erik, and another man, Daniel Gomez."

"And what do we know about Gomez?"

"He works at an insurance broker's in the city. He's been married for three months to Alice Gomez." Carla angled her screen so that Sara could see the man's profile on Facebook.

"Let's see if we can contact him. Get the address of the broker's, you and I will go over there and question him. Also, we need to find out where he lives. I'll let Christine work her magic on that one. I want to get out there and speak to this man ASAP. Christine, look up the address for Daniel Gomez, thanks."

"On it now, boss."

Sara made her way over to the whiteboard and jotted down the details Jeff had given her about the two incidents that had taken place overnight. One thing that struck her when she was making the notes was that Jeff had told her the lorry driver had only seen two people outside the garage, close to the van, not three, as they were led to believe had been involved in the other crimes.

Could the third person already have been inside the van? Had something happened to the third person? Had the gang fallen out with the other member? Or had they been injured in some way during a previous abduction?

"Jill, I know this is going to sound like I'm asking you to search for a needle in a haystack, but I want you to ring the hospital, see if anyone has reported a suspicious injury they have picked up in the last twenty-four to forty-eight hours."

Jill tilted her head. "That could take a while, boss, but I'll crack on with it."

"I know. The reason behind the request is that three members of the gang have suddenly turned into two. We need to find out what has happened to that third member. Yes, there's every chance the other two have dropped them, but let's cover all the angles, just in case."

"Leave it with me, I'll see what I can come up with."

Sara smiled and squeezed her shoulder. "I know you won't let me down." She coughed and called for everyone's attention. "I just want to apologise for my outburst earlier, it was frustration talking. Let's try and rectify things and get this investigation solved swiftly."

Crossing the room to Craig, she tapped him on the shoulder, which startled him. "Sorry to creep up on you. How's it going? Do you need Barry to give you a hand now we have this new information to go on?"

"I'm drowning, or that's how it seems, boss, so any extra help would be appreciated."

"Consider it done. Barry, help Craig, if you would? I need to trace this van today, if possible. Can someone run it through the system? We might not have the numberplate but we have the colour, make and model."

"Can you pass that over to someone else, boss? Scanning the CCTV footage and going through the ANPR cameras is going to put pressure on us."

"Don't worry. Marissa, can I leave that aspect in your capable hands?"

"On it now, boss. I'll see what I can find out."

"Good, I'm glad we're all on the same page at last. Carla, as soon as you've discovered the relevant information about Gomez, we should get on the road."

"Almost there now. Should be free in five minutes or so. I'll give you a shout, if you like?"

As if on cue, Sara's phone rang in her office. "I'll get that. Stick with it."

The phone was answered on its fourth ring. "DI Sara Ramsey," she said breathlessly.

"Ah, Inspector. It's DCI Price. Do you have a spare few minutes to pop along and see me?"

"As it happens, yes. I'll see you soon."

She left her office and announced her intentions as she passed her partner.

"I'll definitely have the information sourced by the time you get back."

"Good."

Sara sprinted along the hallway and entered the secretary's office.

Mary smiled and said, "Go through, she's expecting you. Would you like a coffee?"

"If you wouldn't mind, thanks, Mary."

"My pleasure. I've only just made a pot. I'll bring it in shortly."

Sara knocked on the door and was invited to enter by DCI Price. "Ah, Sara, come in. Is Mary sorting out some coffee for us?"

Sara took a seat. "She is. Is everything all right, ma'am?"

"I don't know, is it?"

Sara frowned but held off asking what the DCI meant by her comment because Mary entered the room with their drinks. She'd also added a shortbread finger to the saucer.

"Thank you, Mary, that will be all," DCI Price dismissed her secretary. "Now, what's all this I've heard on the grapevine about Mark having surgery?"

Sara closed her eyes and chewed her lip. She opened them again to see Price's head tilted to the right.

"Forgive me, I thought I had told you. I can't believe it slipped my mind."

"I'm a little perturbed that you didn't let me know, but I can understand as you must have a lot going on in that head of yours. How is Mark?"

"As far as I know the operation was a success. Umm… he's still in hospital, they're talking about a six-to-eight-week recovery time. I was hoping you would allow me to take some holiday time off at short notice."

"There's no need to ask, you can take as much time as you need, if that's what you both want."

"Knowing Mark, he's going to hate me being around his neck for too long. I should imagine that I'll only need a week or two at the most. I think he'll be back at work within three to four. You know how devoted he is to his customers; it's tearing him apart letting them down with the practice being shut. There's a lack of vets in the area as it is at the moment."

"I recall one of the vets being a victim of a serial killer last year. Tragic incident. I can imagine him chomping at the bit to get back to it. Did the surgery take its toll on him?"

"I visited him last night. He appeared to be in good spirits but fell asleep around twenty minutes after I arrived."

"That's his body telling him he needs to rest. Let's hope he listens to it."

Sara held her fingers up and took a sip from her drink. "Only time will tell. I can see some fraught times ahead of us."

"I don't envy you." Carol laughed, and then her expression turned serious once more. "And how are you coping, running the team? I hear you're dealing with a murder and a missing person investigation at the same time."

"It's been a nightmare week, but things are starting to come together now, thanks to some new information that has come our way overnight."

"Care to share?"

"It's a little early for that, yet. We're making headway, can't we leave things there? I've left the team working diligently, pulling together the different threads we've found."

Carol turned her hands upside down and shrugged. "Is that it? Is that the only clue you're going to offer me?"

Sara smiled. "As soon as we have anything more to go on, you'll be the first to know." She downed the rest of her drink. "Is that all? Only I have people to see and places I need to be."

Carol smiled. "You're a secretive minx at the best of times. I think you've excelled yourself this time, Sara. Stay safe and send Mark my best wishes."

Sara stood and headed towards the door. "I'll do that. Have a good day."

"You, too."

Sara left the office and began her walk back to the incident room. She bumped into Carla coming out of the ladies' toilet.

"Hi, how did it go? Or do you and Mark have something in common now?"

Sara stopped and stared at her. "Is that remark supposed to mean something to me, Carla?"

She shook her head and looked mortified at her choice of words. "I'm sorry, it's something I tend to say now and again. You know, balls getting chewed off. It was in bad taste, wasn't it?"

Sara laughed. "Yes, but I enjoy seeing you wriggle like a worm on the end of a fishing line."

Carla breathed out a relieved sigh. "I thought I had screwed up again."

"Sorry, my fault. I couldn't resist. Are you ready to go?"

"Yes, that first cup of coffee went straight through me. I had to make an emergency stop before we leave."

Sara laughed. "I might need to make a pit stop myself. Be ready to go in five minutes, okay?"

"I will."

THEY DREW up outside the insurance broker's. The car park was full, so Sara found a space at the front of the building instead. She and Carla presented their warrant cards to the middle-aged receptionist who peered at them over her half-rimmed spectacles.

"The police. Oh, and who is it you wish to speak with?"

"Daniel Gomez, if he's around?"

"Ah, sorry. You're out of luck there. He's out for most of the day on appointments. Actually, he's rarely in the office."

"Do you have his itinerary? So we can catch up with him somewhere in between visits."

"I'm not sure if that would be appropriate or not. I would need to run it past my boss first."

"Can you do that? Only time is of the essence as we believe Daniel's life may be in danger."

"Really? Yes, give me a few minutes." She left her desk and entered a door on her right.

The other three people manning the phones in the office all turned their way briefly and then got back to their work.

The receptionist returned. "Mr Atkins said he'd like a word with you before I hand over any sensitive information, if that's all right?"

"It is. Can we see him now?" Sara asked when the woman didn't attempt to let them through to the secure area.

"Sorry, yes, let me assist you. Come to the end, there's an opening there."

She raised the counter which was on hinges, allowed them through, then showed them into Mr Atkins' office. He continued to sit when they entered, his attention caught by whatever was on his screen, until the receptionist cleared her throat.

"These are the police officers I mentioned, Mr Atkins."

Finally, he glanced up, smiled and gestured for Sara and Carla to take a seat. "That'll be all for now, Harriot. Thank you."

The door closed behind the receptionist.

"Now, what's all this about?" he asked and picked up a pen.

Sara watched him wind it through his fingers. "We need to speak with Daniel Gomez as a matter of urgency."

"Yes, yes, Harriot told me that, but I'm going to need you to tell me why before I hand over any personal information to you. I'm sure you of all people would understand the predicament you're putting me in."

"Not really. All we want from you is Daniel's whereabouts at an approximate time. I can't for the life of me understand why you're putting obstacles in our way."

"I'm not. Far from it. It is only my intention to protect my customers' privacy. You've heard of GDPR and the principles behind it, haven't you?"

"Yes, however, I fail to see why that should be of a concern to you."

"Because I will be handing over our customers' addresses without their knowledge."

Sara sighed. "Information that we're not likely to use for anything else, only to track down one of your employees. Are you willing to help us or not? Because we're wasting valuable time here, and as I've already stated, that could result in putting Daniel's life in danger."

"Forgive me, but I run a tight ship around here. I'm law-abiding. I know the police lay traps for people in business now and again. How do I know that this isn't one of your little games, Inspector?"

Sara nudged Carla with her elbow. "I can see we're wasting our time here. If you're insisting we should get a warrant, then I'll willingly oblige. One way or another, we will get the information from you, Mr Atkins." She handed him one of her cards. "Perhaps you wouldn't mind giving Daniel a call, let him know that we would like to have a word with him at his convenience as a matter of urgency, preferably today."

He took the card from her and replied, "Out of the question. I never disturb my staff when they're out on the road. Our customers come first at all times. I'll be sure to pass your card on to him when I see him."

Sara reached the door and with a departing shot, she said, "Let's hope for his sake that's not too late." She didn't wait around to hear what his response might be. "Fucking jobsworth moron. Who the fuck does he think he is?" she muttered, incensed as they wound their way back to the reception area.

"Calm down. He's only doing his job, protecting his customers."

Sara stopped walking and stared at her. "What? Are you coming down on his side? How is that going to help us save Daniel's life?"

"It won't. Let's hope nothing happens to him before we get a chance to speak with him."

"It'll be on that idiot's head if it does. I'll tell you one thing, I won't feel guilty about it."

"Nor should you."

They entered the main office again.

"Oh, that was a quick visit," the receptionist said. "I hope you got what you wanted."

"We didn't, but thanks for your help all the same." Sara raised the counter and slipped through. She didn't bother hanging around to explain her statement to the woman, just left the building.

Carla joined her outside and issued another warning. "Sara, you're going to need to calm down more before I get in the car with you."

Sara took heed of her partner's advice and inhaled and exhaled several deep breaths on the way to the vehicle. "There, all better now. Have we got his home address? We might as well drop by the house on the off-chance that his wife is at home."

"I have it." Carla fished her notebook out of her jacket pocket, and once Sara opened the car doors and turned on the ignition, she input the address into the satnav. "It's not too far. About ten minutes away."

"Suits me. Let's go."

She drew up outside the detached house in Kenchester. "I've not been out this way before, maybe passing through but never actually stopped. It's a nice area."

"Yeah, not bad. My friend used to live out here a few years ago, so I know it quite well. Ah, I think we're in luck, I saw someone upstairs at the front window."

"Let's hope whoever it is wants to speak with us."

They exited the vehicle, and Sara rang the bell. The door was opened a few seconds later by a woman in her late twenties wearing a leisure suit.

"Hello, can I help?"

Sara produced her ID. "Mrs Alice Gomez?"

She frowned and said, "That's right. Is something wrong?"

"We'd like a brief chat with you, if you have time?"

"I was about to embark on my daily yoga session. I suppose I can postpone it for a few minutes. Can I ask what this is about? Sorry, come in, out of the rain. Miserable weather we're having lately. I hope it doesn't flood again like it did in January."

"We're hoping the same, that was terrible for those living by the river. It happens all too often in Hereford, unfortunately. We're trying to track down your husband to have a word with him, but his firm is being very cagey about the information they hand over to us... I mean refusing to give us his itinerary, using GDPR as an excuse."

"That makes sense. I know the boss got into trouble with the authorities regarding that very issue sometime last year, so I can understand his need to be cautious."

"We weren't aware of that. Do you happen to know where your husband is today?"

"I don't, I'm afraid. You're lucky to catch me in, it's my day off. We're due to go out for a meal when he comes home this evening. I refuse to cook when I'm off. I work hard enough as it is during the week."

"I see. What time are you expecting him home?"

"He normally leaves work at five-thirty, give or take a few minutes. Depending how busy the roads are at that time, he gets home about sixish. May I ask why you want to see him?"

"There's no easy way of saying this, but we believe his life might be in imminent danger."

She gasped and covered her mouth with her hand. Once she'd recovered from the shock, she asked, "What do you mean?"

"Is there somewhere else we can talk?"

"Yes, come through to the lounge. I can't believe this."

"I didn't mean to alarm you. That's why it's important for us to speak with him, urgently."

"Of course. And his boss was aware of this fact and still didn't give you the information?"

"That's right. I wonder if you might be able to call him, let him know that we'd like to meet up with him ASAP."

"I know from past experience that when he's out on the road he rarely answers his phone. I know most people will find this hard to believe, but he truly is dedicated to his job, unlike some of his colleagues. He works hard, that's how he achieves lots of bonuses throughout the year. He's the firm's top salesman; the others are quite envious of the number of holidays he wins. We've been to the Maldives, Benidorm and Greece the past three years, and it hasn't cost us a penny."

"How wonderful. Can you at least try phoning him?" Sara asked, not giving two hoots about the man's professional life.

Alice left the room and returned with her mobile. "Sorry, no answer, and I know there'd be no point in me texting him either."

"That's such a shame. Can you tell us what car he drives and the registration number?"

"It's a Ford Kuga, he bought it last year after he received a huge bonus from his boss. I don't know the reg, though, sorry."

"No problem, we can find that out. Sergeant Jameson, can you make the call?"

Carla nodded and left the room.

"What makes you think he's in danger?" Alice asked.

"It's more of a hunch really." Sara withdrew the photo she had saved of the five men on their night out that Carla had spotted on Facebook. "Are you aware of who these people are? Apart from your husband, of course."

"Yes. Do you want me to name them? They go out together maybe once or twice a month, why?"

"There's no need for you to name them, we know who they are. I have to tell you that the other four men have all been abducted this week."

Carla entered the room and retook her seat just as Alice jumped out of hers.

"What? How?"

"We have proof that a blue van has been showing up at different locations, possibly rounding them up. Umm...

unfortunately, one of the men didn't make it, and the gang, the people kidnapping the men, dumped his body in the river."

"Fuck, who was it? Or can't you tell me?"

"It was Ronan Finch."

"Bugger, he was a really nice guy, they all are. What's this gang's motive for abducting them, do you know?"

"We haven't worked that out yet. Can you think of a reason why someone would want to hurt these men?"

Alice returned to her seat. "No, not at all. The thought would never cross my mind."

"Has Daniel shared any concerns with you lately?"

She frowned and shook her head. "About what?"

"Regarding something that might have happened when the group were together, maybe on one of their nights out perhaps?"

"Nothing at all, not from what I can remember. My mind is a little fuzzy, knowing that he might be in danger."

"Try not to be worried. We're doing our best to track him down."

"I know you are and I'm really grateful. I have no way of contacting him, other than if he picks up my text message and calls me back. I doubt if he'll do it and break a habit of a lifetime. What a bloody mess. I feel for Ronan's girlfriend, she's called Lindsay, I believe. She must be devastated by the news of his death. I think they had plans of tying the knot soon, at least, that's what Daniel told me a few months ago. I even went out and bought them an engagement present, it's upstairs, ready for when they hold a party." Her voice drifted off.

"We need to go now, try to find a way of locating your husband, we can do that from our end. I'll leave you one of my cards. If he gets in touch, will you tell him to call me right away? Try not to get him alarmed as it might work against us and scare him."

"Scare him? Why should it do that?"

"He might be too nervous to come home, possibly of putting you in danger, if he's aware of who is abducting the others. At this stage, we're as much in the dark about this as you are."

"Okay, forgive me if I'm not following your logic, though, won't you?"

"I will. All I'm trying to do is keep him safe. If there's nothing else you can tell us then we're going to leave it there for now. Thanks for speaking with us."

"All I can do is keep trying his number. Maybe if I leave enough messages, it'll force him to get back to me. I'll pass on your details if he does."

"And that's all we can ask. Thanks again. Please, try not to worry too much about this."

She showed them to the front door and sighed. "Easier said than done."

Sara smiled and shook her hand. "Stay safe."

"I have every intention of doing that. Are you telling me I might be in danger as well?"

"I don't believe so, but it's better to be safe than sorry."

Alice closed the front door, and Sara heard her attach the safety chain.

"What do we do now?" Carla said. She sounded downbeat.

"We go back to the station and see if we can track Daniel down ourselves." Sara raised a hand as Carla opened her mouth to speak. "Don't ask me how that's going to manifest itself, I haven't got a clue."

"You're not the only one."

. . .

THE AFTERNOON DRAGGED BY. Sara had done all she could. Now it was a matter of sitting back and waiting for Daniel to contact her. They had circulated the details of his vehicle to the patrols in the area, which also meant that if he passed an ANPR camera, they would get alerted.

That alert came in very late that afternoon.

"Right, Craig and Barry, I want you to accompany us to the insurance broker's. He appears to be heading back there to end his shift. He still hasn't contacted me, no idea why that should be."

"Maybe he hasn't picked up his wife's messages," Carla replied.

After Sara and Craig signed out two Tasers, the four of them left the station and battled through the rush-hour traffic to get to the insurance broker's.

Sara's heart all but leapt into her mouth. "Shit, over there, can you see it?"

Carla surveyed the area and shook her head. "Nope. What am I missing?"

Across the road, parked about fifty feet ahead of them, was a blue van. Sara pointed at the vehicle and apprised her colleagues, who were parked in the space behind her.

"Craig, it's me. There's a van over to our left, it could be the one we're after. Keep an eye on it. Don't make any rash moves, we need to ensure it's the right one first."

"We've got it, boss. It's in a strange position if they're intending to pick up Gomez. His car is probably parked round the back in the car park."

"I agree. Wait, it's pulling out of its spot now. Get ready to move. Shit, this could be the break we're looking for."

Sara turned the key in the ignition, and they both ducked when the van drove past. Sara waited a second or two and then drew out of her space and did a U-turn, much to the annoyance of the other drivers surrounding them.

"Fuck off, this is an emergency. Did you see which way they went?"

"Yes, take a left here. That should lead us round the back of the building. I'm sure they went that way."

"Let Craig know."

Carla relayed the information back to their colleagues. The mic clicked twice, signalling they had heard.

Sara came to a stop past the car park, and she and Carla exited the vehicle and joined up with Craig and Barry. Sara poked her head around the corner of the six-foot wall shielding them the possible kidnappers. She saw the van pull into a parking space close to the building. The back door was a few feet away. A member of staff, a female, left the building and spoke to the driver. She walked away, slid into her red sports car and left the area.

"There are two more vehicles left, one is Daniel's Kuga. The other probably belongs to his boss or whoever the keyholder is. Atkins is leaving, hang on, he's with Daniel. This might scupper the gang's plans of abducting him. Yes, Daniel has made it to his car now. Atkins is dealing with the driver of the van. It's reversing, revving its engine and driving off. We need to get back to our cars. We'll follow them."

They scampered back to their vehicles before they were spotted. Sara crossed her fingers that Daniel and the van drove past them instead of going in the opposite direction. Her wish was granted a few seconds later. Daniel whizzed past with the van in hot pursuit. Sara allowed them to get a few feet ahead of her and then pulled out with Craig right behind her, grateful that no other vehicles had got between them.

At the main roundabout, Daniel took the A438 which would eventually lead him home.

"What are you going to do? Wait until they stop or are you going to pull the van over up ahead?"

"I'm winging it at the moment. It would be foolish of us to make a move just yet."

They followed the two vehicles out towards Daniel's house.

When the road appeared to have less traffic, Sara ordered Carla to get Craig and Barry on the radio. "I'm going to make a move, overtake the van, get between them, and then I'm going to slam on the brakes, try and force the van to stop. It might backfire, but I wanted you to be aware of the plan. Hold back a bit, Craig, the last thing we need is you rear-ending the van."

"Roger that, boss. Once the van comes to a halt, do you want us to make a move?"

"Sounds good to me. See you on the other side."

Carla flicked her finger off the mic and turned in her seat to look at Sara. "Are you sure you're going about this the right way?"

Sara shrugged. "We'll soon find out. Brace yourself, and most of all, trust me, I'm not in the habit of putting our lives at risk."

"That's all well and good, but don't forget I've only just returned to work after being injured in the line of duty by a speeding vehicle. I can do without another enforced break, and you have Mark's recuperation to consider as well."

"I know, that's what's going around my head at the moment, well, that and ensuring that Daniel doesn't get abducted, like his friends."

"All right, you've convinced me."

"Keep an eye up ahead, let me know when we go round the next corner if the road is clear of oncoming traffic."

Carla fell silent for the next few seconds until they rounded the bend. "Go, it's all clear."

Sara squeezed her foot down on the accelerator and overtook the van with ease. There was a large enough gap for her to slot between the gang and Daniel's car. The whole manoeuvre turned out to be a walk in the park. The van dropped back a few feet. Sara pounced on the opportunity to make her move. She slammed on the brakes and immediately closed her eyes, preparing herself for impact, but fortunately, the crunch never came. The van slid to a stop behind Sara, veering off at an angle to avoid hitting her. Sara and Carla removed their seatbelts, Sara collected her Taser from the glove box, and they jumped out of the car.

"Switch off your engine and get out of the vehicle," Sara shouted.

They were joined by Craig and Barry. Craig had his Taser drawn, aimed at the passenger side, while Sara kept her weapon trained on the driver.

A discussion seemed to be going on between the driver and the passenger. Actually, it was more like a heated argument. The passenger was the first to open their door and climb out, reluctantly followed by the driver.

The team moved a few paces closer.

Sara wasn't surprised to find the assailants were females, dressed all in black. "On the ground, hands behind your heads where we can see them," she ordered. "Sergeant, can you check if there's anyone else in the van?"

Carla raced towards the rear of the vehicle and quickly returned. "No one else in there."

"Where's your associate? We know there's usually three of you," Sara demanded.

"She dropped out a few days ago," one of the suspects said in a strained voice.

"When you killed Ronan Finch?"

The same woman, the passenger, raised her head, and

with tears in her eyes, she said, "That's right. It was a mistake. We didn't mean to kill him. It was an accident."

"Shut up," the driver shouted at her accomplice.

Sara held up her hand. "Don't say anything else, not until you're under caution, back at the station. Craig and Barry, will you cuff the suspects? We'll separate them, put one in the back of our car."

A car door slammed behind Sara.

A man in his late thirties came rushing towards her. "Were they following me?"

"Are you Daniel Gomez?"

"That's right. Who are you?"

"I'm DI Sara Ramsey. We believe the suspects were about to abduct you and felt it necessary to intervene. We visited your wife earlier; she's been trying to contact you all afternoon regarding what was likely to happen."

"I never answer my phone when I'm at work. I hadn't even noticed if she'd left a message or not, otherwise I would have got in touch. What's this all about?" His gaze drifted over to the suspects who, by now, had been helped to their feet. He gulped.

Watching his reaction, she asked, "Do you know these two women?"

He nodded. "Yes," he whispered.

One of the suspects became restless and attempted to get to him. Craig had to restrain her with more force than he would usually have used.

"You bastard. Murderer. You'll get what's coming to you… one day, I'll make sure of it."

"What are you talking about? You're a nutter, that's why you didn't cop off that night."

Sara listened to the exchange with interest but refrained from intervening.

"You filthy bastard. You knew what you were doing that night... when you raped me."

The colour drained from Daniel's face.

Sara unhooked the cuffs attached to her trousers and flicked them open. "Is this true? Did you rape this woman?"

He glared at Sara for what seemed like eons before he opened his mouth and said, "Of course I didn't. She's mad, surely you can see that?"

"What I'm seeing is that the three of you clearly know each other and something has gone on between you, something bad that has forced these women to abduct four of your friends. You need to come down to the station with us to answer a few questions."

"And if I refuse?"

"Then I'll take that as a sign of your guilt and arrest you. Which is it to be?"

"I'll come but I must go home and speak to my wife first, she'll be anxious."

"Very well. I'll expect you to show up at the station within the hour. If you don't, I will issue a warrant for your arrest."

He stared at her, seemingly dumbstruck by the events, and shook his head. "It was all a grave mistake," he whispered.

"Save it for the interview room, Mr Gomez. I'll see you shortly."

His chin dipped to his chest, and he made his way back to his vehicle.

"Don't let him go, he's going to run, he should be made to pay for what he's done," the woman who had been driving the van shouted, her tone high-pitched, bordering on desperation.

"It's all in hand. Put them in the cars," she ordered Craig and Barry.

Sara stood and watched Daniel get back in his car and continue on his journey to his house.

"Do you think that's what all this is about?" Carla leaned in to ask. "He's guilty of raping her?"

"So it would seem. I don't think we're going to have a problem getting the truth out of them once we're sitting in an interview room."

"Yeah, I was thinking the same. I'll be very surprised if either of the women goes down the 'no comment' route. Saying that, it might have been a different story if Daniel had kept on going and hadn't turned back to find out what was going on."

"I think you're right. Perhaps he's the inquisitive type and it's just backfired on him. Either way, let's head back and get the interviews out of the way tonight. Are you up for that? We'll split up. I'll have Craig in with me to interview the driver, and Barry can assist you with the passenger. My take is that you're going to have the easier time. I think mine will clam up to begin with. I'll need to be smart to worm the information out of her."

"And who is going to have the pleasure of interviewing Daniel, *if* he shows up at the station?"

"I don't mind hanging around to do it. I can ring the hospital in between to see how Mark is doing and visit him later, if it's not too late."

"Are you sure? I don't mind interviewing him."

"You're fine. You have a wedding to prepare for, it's all good."

"And your husband has just had cancer surgery. There's no comparison, Sara."

"I know. It's fine, don't worry about me. Come on, we're wasting time squabbling about it."

Carla laughed. "I wasn't aware that we were."

. . .

"Sit down, Miss Flores. Is it all right if I call you Chelsey?" Sara asked once they had relocated to Interview Room One.

They'd had a brief delay, waiting for two solicitors to show up. The suspects had willingly given their names once they arrived at the station. Which was going to make life easier. She had passed the names to the rest of her team, who had remained on duty. Marissa, Christine and Jill were all going to carry out the background checks on the two suspects and get back to them during the interview if anything important cropped up that they regarded as urgent.

"Whichever is fine by me." Chelsey interlocked her fingers until her knuckles whitened.

"You seem a little uptight, Chelsey, is there any reason for that?"

She glared at Sara and laughed. "Are you for real? Of course I'm uptight, I've just been arrested."

"Not yet, but that will come after we've interviewed you. Perhaps you can tell me why you and your partner, Miss Oliver, were following Daniel Gomez this evening?"

At the sound of his name, Chelsey flinched. She remained silent.

"Come now, you had plenty to say about him when you were pulled over earlier. It would be easier if you told us the truth. How do you know him?"

She inhaled a large breath and held her gaze with Sara. After a long pause, she exhaled and said, "What's the use? You're going to believe his word instead of ours."

"What makes you think that?"

"Because he's a bloke. A salesman with the gift of the gab. He'll have you wrapped around his little finger in no time at all."

Sara smiled and shook her head. "If you believe that then you don't know me. Why don't you tell me why you're so angry with him? Dare I say it? You mentioned he had raped you at the scene this evening, is that true?"

Chelsey's eyes fluttered shut, and her breathing became heavier. Sara watched with interest the way the suspect's chest rose and fell rapidly. Suddenly her eyes flew open, and they were full of tears.

"Yes, of course it's true. I'm not in the habit of lying about something so disgusting, so... demoralising."

"How do you know him?"

"We met on a night out. The two girls I was with were eager to join this group of five men who were showing interest in us. I was outnumbered. It wasn't long before the men were inviting us back to Erik's house for extra drinks and a party."

Sara sat back and listened to her heartfelt story with interest, only asking another question if Chelsey dried up.

"Before long, Polly and Tamzin went their separate ways with their fellas."

"Separate ways? They left the property?"

"No, they ended up in bed with them at the house. Which left me feeling like a spare part. I didn't know any of the men, I don't tend to go around sleeping with guys I don't fancy. Erik gave me a blanket and said I was welcome to spend the night on the couch, alone. When I woke up the next morning..." She swallowed and was struggling to finish her sentence.

"You thought something was different, is that it?" Sara asked.

"I was in my underwear. I wasn't aware of undressing myself. My head was fuzzy. It was then that I realised my drink had been spiked. I presumed whoever had spiked it had also raped me during the night."

"Did you report the rape?"

Chelsey shook her head. "No, I didn't want to cause any friction."

"Any friction?"

"Polly and Tammy were keen on their fellas, continued to see them after that night."

"I'm confused. So, what was the motive behind you going after the group of men and abducting them?"

Chelsey released her hands and clenched her fists together. "I can't say, it's too embarrassing."

"Come now, Chelsey, we need to get to the bottom of why you went out of your way to round these men up and even kill one of them. I'm not saying that rape wouldn't be enough of a motivation for you, which is seriously wrong, but I'm sensing there's more to it than that. If you're hoping for a lesser sentence, then being open and frank with us is the only way you might obtain that."

Chelsey sighed and closed her eyes. When she opened them again, another batch of fresh tears filled them. A teardrop slipped onto her cheek, and she swiftly wiped it away. "All right, you might as well know everything. A few weeks after the incident, I broke out in a rash. I went to the doctor. He shocked me by asking me about my sex life. I was cagey about it, told him I hadn't been with someone since my last boyfriend which was a couple of years ago. He said he wanted to carry out a blood test, fearing that I may have HIV. The results came back positive. Polly, Tammy and I were all in shock. We met up one night, and I had to reveal the truth to the girls. They were both appalled and, between us, we hatched a plan to kidnap the men and carry out a test on them."

"Wow. I know you can buy kits over the counter, is that what you did to test them all?"

"Yes. We kept them at a house out in the country and carried out the tests ourselves, without their knowledge in some cases. All the tests we carried out so far had come back negative. Daniel was the only one left. He has to be the rapist. The one who infected me with HIV."

"And what were you going to do with him if the test came back positive?"

"It would, it has to." Her head lowered, and she mumbled, "I don't know, I hadn't thought that far ahead."

"Okay, let's leave that for a moment. Perhaps you can tell me how Ronan died?"

"It was an accident. We panicked, didn't know what to do with the body, so we threw him in the river."

"An accident. Can you tell me more?"

"Tammy was in charge of knocking him out. She bashed him over the head with the bar. The strike must have been too hard, either that or she hit the wrong part of his head and caused his skull more damage than anticipated. We were all terrified of what would happen to us and decided, as a group, to get rid of the body. We never dreamt that finding his body would lead to this. We saw you put out that press conference, that's how we knew his body had been discovered."

Sara smiled. "Well, it did lead to your downfall, amongst other contributing factors. Where is the third gang member? Polly, is it?"

Again, Chelsey's head lowered. By now, Sara could read her like a book and knew that another key fact was about to emerge.

"She was about to spoil everything. She crumbled and needed to be dealt with to prevent her from speaking to the police."

"Dealt with? As in you silenced her? Have you killed her?"

Chelsey's head rose, and Sara could see the panic in her eyes.

Chelsey waved her hands. "No, no, you don't understand.

She's not dead. I could never kill her, she's one of my best friends."

"Okay, so where is she? At the house along with the men you're holding?"

"No. I kept her at my house. Tammy doesn't know. I couldn't take the risk of Polly being left to roam free with her own confused thoughts going round in her head. She was becoming unstable, liable to spoil the whole plan."

"So, you're holding her captive at your house, is that right?"

Chelsey nodded. "Yes. I repeat, Tammy doesn't know. As far as she's concerned, Polly wanted time apart from us, the space to get her head straight about what was going on."

"And what about the men? Why didn't you release them as soon as you knew they were HIV negative?"

"I couldn't bring myself to do that, not until all the men had been captured and we knew who the culprit was. If I, sorry we, had let any of them go, they would have warned the others, would have been wary of us. Been more cautious. It would have made our lives more difficult. You can understand that, can't you?"

"I can understand your thinking but not the reasoning behind abducting the men and holding them hostage in the first place."

"I'm sorry. It seemed an ideal plan to begin with."

"You've killed one man. Have you harmed any of the others?"

Chelsey's head dropped once more, and Sara prepared herself for yet another possible disturbing revelation. But first she had to prompt the woman for an answer.

"Chelsey, you've been fair and open with us up until now, which will go in your favour when the case goes to court, so you might as well tell us everything."

"I couldn't help myself. I blamed Erik for allowing me to

get raped. It was his house, after all. That was the crime scene. He's a smug bastard. A red mist descended. I tortured him. Polly and Tammy pleaded with me not to, but I couldn't help myself. I felt he was laughing at me. He knew the truth about who raped me that night but refused to reveal who was to blame. Therefore, in my opinion, he deserved to be punished."

Sara sighed. "What did you do to him?"

She repeated the question several times only for Chelsey to shake her head in response.

"I can't tell you. It's too awful."

"Is he still alive?"

"Yes."

"You're going to have to tell us where the house is."

"I can take you there, but I wouldn't be able to give you the address."

"Who can tell us? Tammy?"

"I doubt it. The house belongs to Polly's friend, he's travelling around Australia for six months."

"Then we need to speak with Polly. Give me your address."

Chelsey gave her the information. Sara jotted it down and ordered the constable at the rear of the room to ask the desk sergeant to send a patrol car to the property and to bring Polly to the station. "Will you give me the keys to your house, or shall I tell them to break the door down?"

"No, I handed the keys in, the custody sergeant has them."

"Collect the keys before you speak to the desk sergeant," Sara instructed the constable.

"Okay, ma'am." He left the room.

"Is there anything else you need to tell us, Chelsey, or have we pretty much covered everything?"

"I think that's all. Please, I don't want the other girls to get into trouble. They're good friends who got dragged into this mess."

"But you told me that Tammy was the one who delivered the blow that killed Ronan, that's going to be hard to dismiss."

"Can't you say that I did it? I'm willing to take the fall if it will keep her name out of it. She only had my best interests at heart."

"I refuse to cover up a crime. Your confession has been recorded, you should have thought about the consequences before you mentioned Tammy's name."

Chelsey covered her face and sobbed. "She's going to hate me now."

"She won't. I'm going to arrest you now for abducting four men and for the attempted abduction of Daniel Gomez."

"Okay, I accept the charges. What about Daniel? Will you run a test on him to see if he's the one who raped me and infected me with HIV?"

"Yes, we'll do that, if he agrees."

"Good. I need to know the result when you get it because then I will make an official complaint against him. He won't be able to deny it if the facts are there for all to see."

"That's for the future. First, we need to free the men and get them checked over at the hospital. Let this be a lesson to you. As police officers, we're here to serve the public, to prevent them from taking matters into their own hands. Vigilante justice has no place in our society."

"Tell that to all the women who have reported being raped in the past and who have been let down by the system. Anyway, it wasn't just the rape that we were avenging, it was the fact that Daniel *knowingly* infected me with HIV, effectively giving me a life sentence to deal with."

Sara raised a finger. "That remains to be seen. We'll know

more once he's had the test. Don't worry, if it's positive he won't be allowed to get away with it. I promise you."

Sara concluded the interview and allowed Craig to complete the verbiage for the recording, then asked him to show Chelsey to a cell while Sara nipped next door to see how Carla was getting on with Tammy.

Carla rolled her eyes when Sara entered Interview Room Two. Tammy was sobbing, her head on her arm that was resting on the desk.

The solicitor, Miss Jones, was the first to speak. "It's getting late. I think my client has had enough for now. To be fair, she's answered all your questions and has shown remorse over the death of Ronan Finch."

Sara cocked an eyebrow at Carla, allowing her to decide whether to conclude the interview there or not. She gave a brief nod and left Barry to end the recording.

"Barry, will you escort Tammy to her cell?"

"What? You can't lock me up," Tammy screamed. "I'm not a criminal."

"I'm afraid the evidence plus your confession suggest the opposite is true," Carla said.

Barry and the constable standing at the back of the room helped Tammy to her feet. Her body went limp, and she refused to walk. Tammy was screaming and they were forced to carry her to her cell.

"Well, I didn't expect that," Sara said. "Let's grab a coffee upstairs."

OVER THE NEXT HALF AN HOUR, Sara rang the hospital and spoke to the nurse on duty. She told her that Mark had been in good spirits all day. Sara asked her to pass on her apologies for not being able to visit him that evening. The nurse told her not to worry as Mark was asleep anyway. Which came as a relief to Sara; the last thing she wanted was to let her husband down.

Then she received word from the desk sergeant that Polly had been rescued from Chelsey's house and had been taken to hospital to get checked over. She'd revealed that she was pregnant and feared for the baby's life after the way Chelsey had treated her. She had also given them the address where the three other men were being held hostage.

The next call she received was to inform her that Daniel Gomez had arrived and was ready to be interviewed. Before heading downstairs, Sara dismissed the rest of her team. Carla had insisted she should stay behind and, rather than argue, Sara agreed they should talk to Daniel together.

They entered Interview Room One. Daniel was sitting at the table. Also in attendance was a male constable who stood at the back of the room. Sara and Carla took their seats and started the recording.

"What's this about?" Daniel asked, confused.

"We're interviewing you under caution. We have two witnesses' accounts stating that you raped Chelsey Flores several weeks ago. Is that correct?"

His eyes flicked right then left, and he wrung his hands on the table. "They're lying."

"Okay, they thought you might dispute the charge. Therefore, we're going to ask you to take a voluntary HIV test for us. I have to say, if you refuse, it will go against you."

"What? Why? Is my word not good enough?"

"Not in this case. Will you take the test?"

He huffed out a breath. "Do I have an option? You've made it clear I haven't."

"Thank you. We'll get that sorted, and then you'll be free to go home."

"Is that all there is to it?"

"Yes, for this evening. Once we have the results, we'll be in touch with you in the next day or two."

"I have a question, if you'll answer it?"

"And that is?"

"Why were those women chasing me? What were their intentions?"

"Truthfully? We believe they were going to abduct you and hold you captive with your other friends."

His eyes widened. "What? I can't believe what I'm hearing. Are they all right?"

"My colleagues are on their way to the location now. We'll know soon enough."

He became thoughtful. His expressions changed several times. "Did they say why they kidnapped my friends and attempted to abduct me?"

Sara raised an eyebrow. "Isn't it obvious, in light of what I've asked you for?"

He ran a hand through his hair. "I heard that Ronan died a few days ago, I saw the conference you put out. Did they kill him?"

"Yes, they've admitted his death was down to them but also told us that it was an accident."

"And you believed them? Is that what was on the cards for me and the others?"

Sara shrugged. "I don't think so. All they needed to get to was the truth, and the other men refused to tell them who had raped Chelsey. So, by process of elimination, it was time to come after you."

"I didn't rape anyone, I swear."

"The test will help prove your innocence. I'll get it." Sara left the room to get an HIV test that she'd requested from the desk sergeant.

He quickly ran through what she had to do to obtain the results, and she returned to the room. She opened the box. At first, Daniel pulled back in his chair. Sara wasn't about to give up now, not after coming this far.

She took a step forward, and with the swab in hand, she ordered, "Open your mouth."

It took him a while to comply, and then he opened his mouth half an inch, but not enough for her to gain full access to his gums.

"Wider."

He held her gaze and then closed his eyes, squeezing out a little tear.

Sara completed the test and inserted the swab into the phial to finish the test later. "Go home, Daniel. Don't do anything silly, like trying to abscond. We've got an excellent reputation for tracking down people who attempt to go on the run."

"I won't." He left his seat.

Sara and Carla accompanied him back to the reception area and watched him dart out of the main exit.

"Here's his test. It's going to take twenty minutes until the result comes through. I'm going to shoot off now, I want to nip into the hospital as it's not too late. Can you give me a call with the result?"

"Leave it with me, ma'am. Give Mark our very best wishes."

"I will, if they let me in to see him."

Sara and Carla went back upstairs to collect their belongings, switched off the lights and descended the stairs again.

"I hope for Daniel's sake the test comes back negative," Carla said once they'd left the station.

Sara unlocked her car and paused. "I can't see it myself. He's coming across as shifty to me. You know how I feel about people with characteristics like that."

"I agree. It's been a long day for all of us, don't stay too long at the hospital. Will you text me as soon as you know the result?"

"I will. It might not be immediately if I'm driving but I'll do it as soon as I can. Thanks for staying behind with me this evening, Carla. Enjoy what's left of it."

"I think we'll both sleep easier tonight, knowing that we have the suspects locked up in their cells."

"Amen to that. Goodnight, for now."

"Give my love to Mark."

Sara drove to the hospital and snuck onto the ward. The nurse noted the time on the clock; it was eight-thirty.

"You've missed visiting hours, I'm sorry. The patients need their rest now."

"It's been a busy day, keeping the streets of Hereford safe, arresting criminals. Can I just pop my head in to see him? I promise I won't stay long."

"Switch your phone off and tiptoe down the ward. I'll give you five minutes."

"Thank you." Sara did as instructed and crept alongside Mark's bed. She kissed him on the forehead and watched his eyes flutter open, and a smile appeared on his face. She held a finger to his lips. "We're under strict instructions to remain quiet. I'm sorry I'm late. We arrested two suspects just before we were due to finish our shift. I took the decision to question them tonight."

He smiled. "It's fine. I've been dozing all day and hardly noticed your absence."

"Charming. Any news from the consultant?"

"Yes, they've told me I can come home tomorrow."

She kissed him on the lips. "That's wonderful news. When?"

"Sometime in the afternoon."

"That'll give me time to finish off the paperwork, and then I can take a few days off to care for you."

"Oh, what joy. Does that mean you'll be cooking?" He smiled, the old twinkle back in his eyes.

"What a cheek. Maybe I'll ask the nurse to supply me with a couple of hospital meals instead."

"Okay, you win. I'm only teasing. I've missed you, Sara."

"Not as much as I've missed you. The house has been empty without you being there."

The nurse appeared at the end of the bed and tapped her watch.

"I have to go. Give me a call tomorrow, and I'll come and pick you up."

They shared another kiss, and Sara accompanied the nurse back to her station.

"Thank you for allowing me to see him."

"It's a pleasure. Did he tell you we're letting him home tomorrow?"

"He did. I'm so grateful for all you've done for him."

"He still has a way to go yet. We're trusting you to ensure he receives the rest and recuperation he needs over the next couple of weeks."

"I'll see that he gets it, even if I have a fight on my hands. He's not the type to sit and watch TV all day."

"Are any of us, when we're forced to?"

"I suppose not. Goodnight, thanks again for letting me in to see him."

Sara switched her phone back on to find a text message from the station. The result was in... positive. She punched the air and took the stairs down to the ground floor. In the car, before she drove home, she texted Carla to let her know. Carla sent a huge thumbs-up in response and added a heart.

EPILOGUE

In the end, Sara took the next two weeks off work. Mark turned out to be a nightmare patient to care for, and they fell out a few times, especially when she caught him sneaking out of the house to go to the practice. Sara had needed a visit to their GP to emphasise to Mark how important it was that he spent the time recovering and not thinking about his business, which turned out to be easier said than done.

At the end of the two weeks' recuperation period, Mark's strength had improved considerably, enough to allow them to attend Carla and Des' wedding.

It was a reasonably quiet celebration. Family and friends turned up at the registry office to witness the ceremony. Carla was dressed in a stunning cream silk trouser suit, and Des looked equally fetching in the wedding suit he'd hired.

The reception was held at a local hotel, a buffet with enough food to feed a hundred people, instead of only the twenty who had been invited.

Carla caught Sara coming out of the ladies' toilet. "I'm so

glad you and Mark could make it. He's looking incredibly well, considering what he's been through."

"He's getting there. I have to admit, he's driven me to the edge and back again at times, but we've got through it. The doctor is delighted with his progress and has even told him that he can go back to light duties at the practice next week."

"So, no lifting fifteen-stone St Bernards onto his table for an examination then?"

They both laughed.

"Ouch, even the thought of him doing that is bringing tears to my eyes."

"Mine, too. And there's no need for you to be concerned about work either, I've coped admirably while you've been off this time. You'll have no dreaded post cluttering up your desk, no more than the usual that comes in the night before. I thought I'd better add that part, in case you take me at my word."

"Has it been quiet in my absence?"

"Too quiet. Not wanting to talk shop, but I need to tell you this snippet of information. After receiving the result, Craig and I nipped out to arrest Daniel. He's still maintaining that he didn't lay a finger on Chelsey that night, but the facts are there for all to see. His wife was none too happy. She packed her bags and has gone to stay with her parents until the trial is over."

"Good. Men like that disgust me. Did he admit to having HIV, or did the news come as a shock to him?"

"He said he didn't know, but there was a glint in his eye. His wife was mortified as they had been trying for a baby. She took the test, too, and it came back positive."

"The *bastard*. So effectively, he's ruined three lives, including his own. Did he reveal where he likely picked up the disease?"

"It took us a while to get the truth out of him but, eventually, he admitted that he'd picked a girl up at a nightclub on his stag night and, get this, he found out later that she was a prostitute."

"Jesus, does that man have no shame?"

"Hard to fathom, eh?"

"Sorry, I know this is supposed to be your wedding day, we must keep reminding ourselves of that, but what happened to the men they rescued from the house?"

"The only one who had any severe injuries was Erik Pittman. One of his fingers had to be amputated as half of it was missing. They found the piece that had been snipped off, but it was too late to stitch it back on."

Sara shuddered. "Oh my. That man must have been in agony."

"He also took a battering to his legs. They were both broken in numerous places. He also had a couple of busted ribs and needed hours of surgery to put everything right."

"Bugger. And the other men?"

"They got off lightly, but who's to say what might have happened to them if we hadn't intervened when we did?"

"It doesn't bear thinking about, does it?"

"Are you two talking shop?" Des snuck up behind them.

"Only a teensy bit. My fault entirely," Sara said. She leaned in and planted a kiss on his cheek. "Congratulations. I knew you two were made for each other the minute I laid eyes on you."

Des hooked his arm around Carla's shoulder. "I'm the luckiest guy alive."

"No, I think I am." Mark slid his arms around Sara's waist.

She twisted in his arms and kissed him. "You say the nicest things. I'm surprised we haven't murdered each other over the past couple of weeks."

He winked at her and said, "The day is still young."

The four of them laughed. A waitress passed by with a

tray of champagne flutes. She stopped and offered them a glass.

Des passed the drinks around, and Mark proposed a toast.

"To good friends and to a love that will be tested to its limits at times. Good luck, Carla and Des."

"I'll second that," Sara said. "Happy wedding day, and to all the good times ahead of you."

THE END

THANK you for reading Seeking Retribution, Sara and Carla's next adventure can be found here **Gone...But Where?**

HAVE you read any of my fast paced other crime thrillers yet? Why not try the first book in the award-winning Justice series Cruel Justice here.

OR THE FIRST book in the spin-off Justice Again series, Gone In Seconds.

WHY NOT TRY the first book in the DI Sam Cobbs series, set in the beautiful Lake District, To Die For.

PERHAPS YOU'D PREFER to try one of my other police procedural series, the DI Kayli Bright series which begins with The Missing Children.

. . .

Or maybe you'd enjoy the DI Sally Parker series set in Norfolk, Wrong Place.

Or my gritty police procedural starring DI Nelson set in Manchester, Torn Apart.

Or maybe you'd like to try one of my successful psychological thrillers She's Gone, I KNOW THE TRUTH or Shattered Lives.

KEEP IN TOUCH WITH M A COMLEY

Pick up a FREE novella by signing up to my newsletter today.
https://BookHip.com/WBRTGW

BookBub
www.bookbub.com/authors/m-a-comley

Blog

http://melcomley.blogspot.com

Why not join my special Facebook group to take part in monthly giveaways.

Readers' Group

Printed in Great Britain
by Amazon